RANGER INTEGRITY

TEXAS RANGER HEROES

LYNN SHANNON

CT
Creative Thoughts

RANGER INTEGRITY

Copyright © 2023 by Lynn Balabanos

Published by Creative Thoughts, LLC

This book is a work of fiction. Names, characters, businesses, organizations, places, events and incidents either are the product of the author's imagination or are used factitiously. Any resemblance to actual persons, living or dead, events, or locales is entirely coincidental.

Cover design by Maria Spada.

Scripture appearing in this novel in whole or in part from THE HOLY BIBLE, NEW INTERNATIONAL VERSION®, NIV® Copyright © 1973, 1978, 1984, 2011 by Biblica, Inc.™ Used by permission. All rights reserved worldwide.

Be kind and compassionate with each other, forgiving each other, just as in Christ God forgives you.

Ephesians 4:32

ONE

Was she making a terrible mistake?

Sienna Evans hesitated, her fingers on the gearshift. The bright beam of her headlights cut across the mostly empty parking lot, illuminating the chain-link fence topped with barbed wire. Beyond the gate, moonlight gently caressed the ocean water, and the boats moored in the marina. It was nearly midnight. Not another soul in sight. Exactly what Albert Greer was hoping for.

The fisherman was jittery when he'd phoned earlier in the day claiming to have information about a missing person's case. Ruby Morales. The police hadn't located the twenty-two-year-old administrative assistant, but that hadn't stopped Sienna from taking the case. As a private investigator, she rarely said no. Persistence and determination helped her succeed where the police failed. She'd find an overlooked clue, or more often than not, a witness who refused to speak to authorities would provide information to her.

Someone like Albert. Given his criminal history, Albert wasn't fond of law enforcement. He'd insisted on meeting Sienna on his boat in the marina. The rusty vessel wasn't designed to be a house, but Albert had recently been evicted from his apartment and was temporarily crashing there.

Sienna suspected the sly fisherman wouldn't give her the low-down until she'd slipped him some cash. She'd stopped by the ATM on her way to the marina. Her bank account was running dangerously low, but money was a small price to pay if it meant uncovering the truth about what'd happened to Ruby. The young woman had been missing for three weeks, and while most victims were killed within hours of their abduction, there was evidence Ruby was alive and being held captive. Albert's information could break the case wide open. Sienna prayed it would.

Lord, please guide my words and actions. Help me convince Albert to share what he knows.

Fortified, Sienna killed the engine of her SUV and exited the vehicle. Wind whipped through her thick mane of curls. Goosebumps pebbled on her skin, and she quickly zipped up her coat. January in Sandalwood, Texas didn't bring snow, but temperatures dropped at night and the ever-present humidity added a dampness to the cold that cut right to the bone.

Loose gravel crunched under her boots. The entrance gate to the marina was cracked open, exactly as Albert had promised it would be. Sienna slipped inside the fence line. The boat rental office was dark, as was the tackle supply shop. Her footfalls were silent as she stepped off the pavement and onto the floating dock. The wood and steel structure shifted underneath her, gently rocked by the waves rippling across the water.

Boats of every shape and size rested in their slips. She passed several dinghies, a few speedboats, and a houseboat before turning toward the industrial side of the marina. Small fishing vessels lurked in the water, hidden from the moonlight by several warehouses built on the shore. At one time, Sandalwood maintained a healthy fishing community. Industrialization and large conglomerates had driven most of the independent fishermen out of business. A few, like Albert, hung on though.

The darkness enveloped her as Sienna followed the floating dock to a remote area of the marina. The eerie sense of being watched tickled the back of her neck. She turned and looked. A shadow slipped into one of the nearby warehouses.

Was she being followed?

Or worse, was Albert setting her up in some way? What if he had something to do with Ruby's disappearance and was luring Sienna here for nefarious purposes? The thought sent a chilling spiral of fear coursing down her spine. She hadn't uncovered a connection between Albert and the missing woman, but her investigation was in its early stages.

Her ex-fiancé's frequent warning popped into her mind.

Refusing to play by the rules may get you killed.

Eli had always delivered the words with his trade-mark scowl, normally after discovering some risk she'd taken in pursuit of justice. Sienna never heeded his words. She couldn't. The families that hired her were desperate for answers, and she knew firsthand what it was like to be left praying for answers. Her own sister's murder case had lingered unsolved for years before Sienna finally caught the killer. She refused to let another family go through that pain.

Some things are worth the risk.

That had always been her reply to Eli, right before planting a kiss on his lips to erase the worry etched on his handsome features.

It'd been five years since they'd last spoken. Not since they'd broken up. A pang of sadness tangled with regret at the turn their relationship had taken. She shoved it back. It was better Eli had walked away. Marriage would've meant a lifetime of compromise with a man who didn't see the world in the same way she did. At the very least, he would've urged her to take fewer risks.

Like this one.

Sienna glanced over her shoulder again. This time, nothing stirred. Nerves jittered her insides, signaling some unknown danger she couldn't see. Or maybe she was simply creeped out by the dark buildings, the soft lap of the water against the hulls, and the eerie scent of rotten fish floating in the air. The shadow she'd seen earlier could've been a figment of her imagination.

It probably had been. Creeping around the marina in the dead of night was enough to give anyone the willies. Especially since her primary suspect in Ruby's disappearance had a houseboat on the other side of the large and intricate floating dock. Sienna didn't have proof Dallas Redding had anything to do with the young woman's kidnapping, but she hoped Albert might be able to shed some light on his fellow seaman's whereabouts on the night Ruby went missing.

Then again, Albert might lie through his teeth from the beginning of his statement to the last. He wasn't a trustworthy individual. He'd been arrested for blackmail and fraud. Violence wasn't part of his criminal past, but still... people could be surprising.

Sienna's fingers brushed against the small of her back before she remembered her holster wasn't there. Her Glock had been stolen this afternoon from the glove box of her SUV while she'd visited her father at the hospital. He'd suffered from a heart attack three days ago. Thankfully, he was on the mend, but the hours in surgery and the days since had been emotionally draining for everyone in her family.

Coming out of the hospital and seeing her SUV's broken window was a complication she hadn't needed. The thief had stolen her radio, her handgun, and her battery. All things that were easy to sell. Sienna couldn't have cared less about the radio and the battery. Those could be replaced easily.

The stolen Glock was a different matter altogether.

Guns were sold on the black market to criminals who later used them to commit horrible deeds. She'd immediately reported the theft to the local police department. Then placed calls to the local pawn shops in the slim chance the engraved weapon was sold for immediate cash. No such luck.

Sienna was trained in karate and could hold her own in a hand-to-hand fight, but it was times like these, she appreciated having her Glock as well. Although there was no obvious sign of danger, it was hard to shake the feeling of foreboding crawling across her skin.

Ropes creaked as she drew closer to Albert's fishing vessel. The street lamps were a distinct memory, the only illumination a faint light emanating from the cabin below deck. The mast, even without its sails, cast a long shadow. A muffled plop emanated from the water. It skated along the edge of Sienna's heightened nerves. She peered into the darkness at the far end of the boat. "Albert?"

Her voice was hushed but strong enough to carry across the distance.

Silence answered.

Once again, the weighted sensation of eyes watching her swept across Sienna. Her heart rate picked up speed. The warehouses lurked on the shore like ghostly sentries. A person could be hiding nearby and she wouldn't know. It sent her nerves jittering. She didn't like this. A part of her was tempted to abandon this risky meeting, but Sienna shook off the urge. Ruby's grandmother was worried sick about her only grandchild. She deserved answers.

Sienna intended to get them.

There was no movement above deck. Albert was likely inside the cabin. Annoyed and cold, Sienna stepped onto the fiberglass hull. The deck was cluttered with paraphernalia. A pile of fishing nets clawed at her foot and she tripped trying to wrench it free. Her body slammed into the deck with a teeth-clattering jolt. Slime and salt water seeped into her clothes. Repulsed, she scrambled onto her hands and knees. "Albert!"

No movement from inside the cabin. Irritation flared white-hot. She was exhausted after a long day of work, creeped out by the clandestine meeting in the marina, and now was covered in leftover fish goo and salt water.

Sienna gritted her teeth and pulled her foot free of the net before standing. Her hands clenched. She shouldn't let her emotions get the best of her, but Albert was in for several choice words if he'd dragged her out here for nothing.

Sucking in a breath, Sienna carefully crossed the slick distance between the edge of the boat and the cabin. The helm was nothing more than a few instruments and a steering wheel. A door led to a small interior area below deck.

She pushed it open, revealing a set of narrow stairs. Music spilled from the cabin. Body sweat and the faint hint of blood wafted across her nose. Sienna grimaced. It smelled like Albert was cleaning fish in the same place he was sleeping. Yuck.

A counter ran along the edge of the cabin. It was covered with various items. A hotplate rested next to a jagged knife. Hooks and fishing line mingled with discarded cans of soup. As Sienna descended the staircase, Albert came into view. He reclined in a fancy camping chair with a footrest attached. His eyes were closed, hands propped up on his lap.

For some ridiculous reason, the sight of him sleeping fueled her frustration and irritation. Sienna flicked off the nearby radio. "Wake up, Albert."

He didn't stir.

Sienna lifted her fingers to her mouth in preparation to whistle sharply, when something about his positioning stalled her movements. Dread slicked through her like a heat wave. She slowly lowered her hand to his shoulder. His skin was warm to the touch, even through the fabric of his shirt. Sienna shook him.

Albert pitched from the chair, nearly falling into her as he toppled to the floor.

Sienna recoiled. The back of Albert's head was covered in blood. A dark stain coated his collar and the backside of his T-shirt.

Bile rose in the back of her throat as her backside slammed into the counter. The soup cans rattled. A bobbin toppled to the floor. It rolled slowly to the side of Albert's arm. Her gaze followed its path. She'd seen crime scene photographs, but had never been in the presence of a dead body before. Horror swallowed her up and stole her breath. Her knees weakened. She couldn't tear her attention away from the back of Albert's head. It looked like he'd been shot.

A thump came from overhead.

The noise sliced right through Sienna's shock. It sent her heart rate skittering as terror took hold. Albert's killer. Had he come back?

Another scuffle overhead. Someone was definitely on the deck. Panic shot straight through Sienna as instinct took over. She searched the small space for something to use as a weapon. Her gaze snagged on a dark object on the floor.

A gun. A Glock 19.

She moved closer, her pulse roaring in her ears as she recognized the familiar engraving on the grip. The initials S.E. enclosed inside a round circle topped with a cross.

Her initials.

Her gun.

Her *stolen* gun.

Dizziness threatened to swallow her whole as black edges appeared at the corners of her vision.

More movement on the deck drew her gaze upward. Survival instinct overtook logic as Sienna scooped up the Glock from the floor of the cabin. She quickly ejected the magazine. One bullet was missing.

She didn't want to think about where that bullet was. Not now. Instead, she snapped the magazine in place, her movements smooth despite the fear coursing through her veins.

Whoever murdered Albert wouldn't hesitate to harm Sienna. The only escape route was through the wooden cabin door, but she'd never make it outside without being noticed. She prayed whoever was on the boat wouldn't come below deck.

The steps grew louder, thumping against the hull like a herd of elephants. Growing closer.

She kept the gun pointed at the cabin door. Said another prayer. Held her breath.

And waited.

TWO

He swore he'd never talk to her again.

Texas Ranger Elijah "Eli" Goodwin leaned against his truck. An overcast sky matched his dour mood, his gaze locked on the exit of the Sandalwood Police Department. The short, squat building was at the edge of town next to a diner and across the street from the courthouse. Several brave pedestrians battled the frigid weather to hop in and out of the specialty shops running down Franklin Street before closing time. Eli barely registered the activity happening along the periphery of his vision. His attention was locked on the mirrored exit door, his mind trying to process the turbulent emotions rolling his insides.

Any moment, Sienna Evans would be released from the holding cell. His ex-fiancée. The woman who'd broken his trust and shattered his heart. Eli swore he'd never talk to her again after their breakup five years ago. He'd promised himself and the good Lord above to stay away from her. But what was that saying? If you want to make God laugh, tell him your plans.

Well, He must be having quite the chuckle. Because here Eli was, bailing his ex out of jail, waiting for her to explain how she'd gotten messed up in a murder charge.

His cell phone vibrated. Eli pulled the device from his pocket, glancing at the screen. Ryker Montgomery. His best friend and a fellow Texas Ranger. They were supposed to have dinner tonight, but that wasn't happening. Eli hit the answer button. "Hey. Guess you got my text."

"Sure did. What's going on?"

"Sienna was arrested for murdering a local fisherman by the name of Albert Greer. Police received an anonymous phone call reporting the sound of gunshots coming from Albert's boat. Officers arrived on the scene and found Sienna standing over the man's dead body, holding a Glock. *Her* Glock. They arrested her. I've posted bond, and I'm waiting for Sienna to come out of the police station." He heaved out a breath, the air fogging in front of his face. "It doesn't look good, Ryker. Ballistics confirm the bullet that killed Albert came from Sienna's gun. She reported it stolen from her SUV's glove box yesterday while she was visiting her father in the hospital."

Eli had been distressed to learn Wyatt Evans suffered from a heart attack last week. He was doing okay now, but the stress of having his daughter arrested for murder couldn't be good for him.

"The police doubt her story?" Ryker asked.

"Considering they found her standing over a dead

body holding the murder weapon in her hand... yep. They think she faked the theft to cover her tracks because she was planning to murder Albert later that night. Apparently, Albert blackmails folks. The police believe that's her motive, since Sienna had several hundred dollars in cash on her at the time of her arrest."

Ryker scoffed. "Sienna wouldn't kill a blackmailer. She'd get evidence proving the crime, so the police arrest the guy."

His good friend's words solidified Eli's own feelings on the matter. Which is why he'd hopped in his truck and driven the one hundred miles to Sandalwood immediately after receiving the call from Sienna's mother. It didn't matter that his ex had betrayed him. Or that Eli had promised never to have communication with her again. He wouldn't let Sienna go to prison for a crime she didn't commit.

"She won't get a fair shake from the police chief." Eli removed his cowboy hat from his head and pressed the heel of his palm against his forehead. A headache was brewing. Too much coffee and not eating all day was a terrible combination. "Sienna and the Sandalwood Police Department have a contentious relationship. They have been from the beginning of her career. She's embarrassed them over and over again, solving cases they couldn't, starting with her own sister's."

Harper had been murdered by her ex-boyfriend in a drug-fueled rage during a party in the woods. The case had remained unsolved until Sienna uncovered the killer's identity, along with Eli's help. Back then, he'd been the Texas Ranger for this area. Her passion for justice coupled with her strong family values and incredible good looks had smashed through every one of Eli's walls. He'd fallen madly in love with the fiery brunette.

And then everything fell apart.

Eli replaced the cowboy hat on his head. "I've spoken several times to Sienna's defense attorney. Albert's murder is connected to a case Sienna's working on, although I don't have all the details. This isn't exactly how I imagined spending the last few weeks of my medical leave, but... there you go."

Eli had been shot in the line of duty several months ago, and the road to recovery had been slow. The doctors promised he'd be cleared to return to work in a few weeks. His nose wrinkled thinking of it. Desk duty is what they meant. He hated paperwork. "Anyway, I'll keep you updated when I find out more."

"Good. I'll reach out to Cole Donnelly in the meantime. He has a good working relationship with the chief. Maybe Cole can convince him to allow the Texas Rangers to aid in the investigation."

Local law enforcement always had primary jurisdiction over murders, but could invite the Texas Rangers to assist in tough cases. Most departments were grateful for the help. Eli doubted the chief would accept their offer to assist. Chief Boone Ramirez was territorial about his cases. Still, it was worth a try. "Appreciate it."

Just as Eli hung up, the exit door of the county jail swung open. Sienna stepped onto the sidewalk. She'd spent the night and most of the day in jail. Her wild curls were tangled and worry lines creased her forehead. The oversized sweatsuit swallowed her athletic frame. Still, Eli's breath hitched.

It'd been five years since he'd last seen her, and the circumstances were less than ideal, but it didn't matter. She was the most beautiful woman he'd ever clapped eyes on. His first instinct was to close the distance between them and wrap her in his arms. And he hated himself for it.

This. This is why he'd steered clear of her after their breakup. His mind knew there was no future with her, but his heart had never fully absorbed the message.

Her gaze locked with his. Surprise didn't flicker across her face. They hadn't spoken since her arrest, but her defense attorney had run messages back and forth. Sienna knew her parents had called him. That he'd posted the bail to get her out of jail. Wariness tangled with the amber flecks buried in her hazel eyes.

He strolled toward her. The pain and anger and attraction tangled inside him like a tornado threatening to whip out of control, but he smashed it down. There was no need to discuss their past. Her betrayal. Their breakup. The only issue that mattered was the murder.

As he drew closer, she took a giant step back, holding up a hand to ward him off. "Stay there. I smell like rotten fish and sour beer. Forensic technicians took my clothes into evidence, but they wouldn't let me take a shower to rid myself of the muck from the boat." Her nose wrinkled. "Then my drunk cellmate was sick everywhere. I'm dying for a shower."

"I'm sure." The breeze shifted, and Eli's eyes watered at the stench wafting from Sienna's clothes. She hadn't been kidding about the stink. His mouth quirked up. "We'll keep the windows rolled down."

Her gaze skittered from his. "Where's Isabella? I thought she'd be here."

Isabella Gomez was Sienna's best friend. Also her defense attorney. The two women had known each other for years and often worked together.

"Something came up," Eli explained. "An emergency on another case. I'm your ride home."

"There's no need. I live fifteen blocks from here. I'll just walk."

"That's a terrible idea. You've been charged with murder. Sandalwood gossip is running high at the moment, and you won't make it five steps without a neighbor interrogating you about what happened. Besides, there are things we need to talk about."

He marched to his truck and opened the extended cab, removing an emergency blanket from his first aid kit. He spread it over the passenger seat before gesturing for Sienna to get in.

She didn't move, her shoulders tense, chin remaining at a stubborn angle. "There's nothing for us to discuss." Sienna sucked in a breath as if she'd rehearsed this next part. "I appreciate you driving all the way to Sandalwood and posting my bond. I'll pay you back as soon as possible, but there's no need to involve yourself further. My parents shouldn't have called you in the first place, and I'll make sure they don't bother you again."

"Don't be stubborn. You need my help."

She crossed her arms over her chest. "I'm perfectly capable of figuring things out on my own. Frankly, I'm surprised you're here at all."

Buried in her tone was a hint of accusation. He couldn't blame her for it. Bailing people he cared about out of jail was something Eli normally refused to do. A fact his brother, Dalton, learned the hard way.

His younger brother had been a troublemaker since childhood. An abusive father and a depressed mother made for a challenging combination. Eli relied on rules and regulations to steer his life in the right direction and tried to help his brother do the same, but Dalton rebelled against any kind of authority.

As a teen, after both of their parents passed away, he came to live with Eli. Their relationship soured by the day. Dalton was hanging with the wrong crowd, doing drugs, and skipping school. At twenty-three, Eli had been ill-prepared to deal with a rebellious and hurting sixteen-year-old. They fought. Often. Not even dragging Dalton to church made any difference. His brother was determined to screw up his life as much as possible.

Finally, after years of heartache, Dalton agreed to go to rehab. It wasn't cheap, but Eli used every penny in his savings account to pay for it.

Dalton came home six months later. Eli was a newly minted Texas Ranger at the time, and while he wouldn't allow Dalton to live with him, he paid for an apartment in the same complex. His brother got a job working construction. They started hanging out together. It seemed Dalton was finally on the right track.

Until one fateful night, he stole Eli's truck to buy drugs. High and drunk, he slammed into an elderly couple coming home from a church social. No one was seriously hurt, but Dalton was arrested at the scene.

It was the final straw for Eli. He was done. When Dalton called from jail, begging to go back to rehab, Eli hung up on him.

At the time, Sienna and Eli were engaged. She attempted to convince Eli to help Dalton. He refused. The next day, she bailed Dalton out and drove him there herself.

It was a betrayal. For Eli, an unforgivable one. He broke off their engagement and never spoke to her again.

So yes, it was surprising he was here now, but there was one big difference between Sienna and Dalton.

Dalton had been guilty of the crime he'd been arrested for.

Sienna, however, was innocent.

Eli's hand tightened on the passenger side door as he met her gaze. "Your parents called me for a reason. They're worried about you. Scared, if truth be told."

Her complexion paled slightly. No one mattered more to Sienna than her family. She was one of the most loyal people Eli had ever met. It was one of the reasons her betrayal all those years ago had stung so much. He'd never thought in a million years that she'd go behind his back to do something he'd expressly rejected.

"You're in a heap of trouble," Eli continued. "The

evidence the police have uncovered so far makes you look guilty. So do you want to spend the rest of your life in prison for a murder you didn't commit?" He jabbed a finger toward the passenger seat. "Or are you going to get into this truck and tell me what happened so I can help get you out of this mess?"

THREE

Forty minutes later, Sienna was still debating the wisdom of accepting Eli's ride home.

She eyed her reflection in the bathroom mirror. Dark circles hung like half moons under her eyes and her cheeks appeared gaunt. A hot shower and a fresh change of clothes had washed away the grime of the last twenty-four hours, but nothing could erase the image of Albert's dead body from her mind. Someone had murdered the man in cold blood. And framed her for the crime. Eli wasn't wrong when he said she was in serious trouble, but his unexpected arrival and offer of help was a complication she didn't need.

Five years. They hadn't spoken in five years. Not for lack of trying on her part. She'd called him a few times, but her messages were ignored. Then this past Christmas, she'd sent him a Get Well letter after hearing he'd been shot in the line of duty.

Silence had been his response.

It'd left a bitter taste in her mouth. Yes, they'd parted on bad terms, but there had once been love between them. Did Eli despise her so much he couldn't even send her a Christmas greeting? And if so, why show up now?

More importantly, why provide the money to bail her out of prison? Not that Sienna wasn't grateful. She was. Bail had been set at $100,000. A bondsman would require 10% of that in cash. It was an insurmountable amount for Sienna. She hadn't become a private investigator for the money and often took cases even when the clients couldn't pay much. Who could turn away a mother desperate to find her missing child? Or a family seeking answers about their loved one's murder? Not her.

Instead, she'd been frugal. She rented a tiny bungalow, which also housed her office, and that kept costs low. While she had some funds in her emergency savings account, it wasn't enough to satisfy the bail amount. Normally, her family would rally around her, but they'd also fallen on hard times. Several years of poor crops required her parents to take out a second mortgage on their farm, and her father's recent health troubles had drained their savings. Her brother lived and worked on the farm as well. He'd poured his own meager savings into repairing old equipment so they could finally turn a profit this year.

Before Eli arrived, she'd been facing weeks or months in jail, waiting for her parents to raise the bail money. A horrible thought. Behind bars, Sienna was useless. She couldn't prove her innocence locked inside a metal cage.

So, while she was grateful for Eli's actions, his decision to help was confusing.

It simply didn't make sense. And it was foolish to believe they could work together without the past rearing its ugly head. With a missing woman to find and a murder charge hanging over her, Sienna didn't have the time or the energy to navigate their problematic relationship.

She flicked off the light to the bathroom and padded on thick socks out of the bedroom. The heavenly scent of warm cheese wafted from the ground floor. Her stomach rumbled. She hadn't eaten since yesterday. Sienna's steps quickened and her breath caught as she rounded the corner to the kitchen.

Eli stood at the stove. His sunshine blond hair was ruthlessly trimmed short and, although it was nearing dinnertime, his jawline was clean-shaven. He'd shed his coat, revealing a flannel shirt underneath that molded to broad shoulders before skirting the ridges and planes of his back. Jeans, worn soft by the years, hung from his narrow hips. One strong hand held a spatula.

It was disconcerting and far too intimate to have Eli standing at her stove. Memories flooded Sienna's mind before she could stop them. Laughter as they danced around the kitchen, long conversations spent over delicious dinners, nights curled up on the couch watching movies. Longing mixed with regret rattled her already frayed emotions. "You didn't need to cook."

"I was hungry. Figured you were too."

Her gaze swept across the clean sink and the organized mugs next to the coffee maker. That was not how she'd left the kitchen. Sienna's gaze narrowed. "Did you clean?"

"A bit." With precision, Eli flipped the sandwich roasting in the frying pan. The first side was already perfectly golden. "I found tomato soup in your pantry. Hope that's okay."

Sienna glanced at the small table in the corner. Bowls of soup rested on placemats, along with silverware and glasses filled with water. Her stomach growled in anticipation. She pressed a hand to her midsection as a heat flushed her cheeks.

Eli chuckled before sending her a wink. "Sit down. Start eating, if you want. The sandwiches are almost ready."

He was taking care of her, and although Sienna knew she shouldn't allow it, exhaustion prevented her from launching a defense. She sank into the nearest chair. A quick prayer of thanks to God was all her brain could manage before she reached for the spoon.

The soup was thick and warm, flavored with summer tomatoes and a hint of spices. A secret recipe. Eli knew how to take a simple can of tomato soup and turn it into a culinary masterpiece.

She'd missed it. Missed him.

Dangerous thoughts.

Sienna scooped another spoonful of soup into her mouth. "It's delicious. Thank you."

Eli set a plate topped with a grilled cheese sandwich at her elbow. Then he joined her and said a quick prayer before picking up his own spoon. "Nothing fancy, but it'll do the trick." He wrinkled his nose. "You don't have much in the fridge."

"I don't cook very often."

"Probably for the best." His grin was lopsided. "I vaguely remember a flaming pot roast and a desperate run for a fire extinguisher."

Not her finest moment. Sienna laughed. She reached for her sandwich and dipped a corner into the bowl of tomato soup. "I'm too busy working most of the time to cook. Besides, Mom and Dad invite me to dinner four nights a week anyway. Now that Landon is living on the farm again, they like seeing us."

Sienna didn't mind spending a lot of time with her parents and her brother. They were close-knit, made more so by the untimely death of her older sister.

She swiped at her mouth with a napkin. "Speaking of family, how is Ryker? I heard through the grapevine that he got married last year."

Technically, Ryker wasn't Eli's blood relative, but the two men were as close as brothers. They'd grown up together, and as far as Sienna knew, Eli didn't have any other family. Other than Dalton, of course. But that wasn't a subject she was ready to tackle.

"Ryker's well. Yes, he got married. His wife, Hannah, is amazing and they're expecting a baby in the fall." Eli's tone was full of affection and love. "A little boy. I've suggested the name Elijah, but they aren't making any promises."

Sienna laughed. "Maybe they'll make you the godfather instead."

The smile that stretched across Eli's face caused a riot of butterflies in Sienna's stomach. Happiness took his already handsome features and morphed them into something breathtaking. A faint dimple creased his left cheek. Sienna couldn't resist staring. Drinking him in like a woman starved for affection. And before she could stop herself, the question hovering in the back of her mind was out of her mouth. "Are you dating anyone?"

He stilled for half a moment. "No." Eli cleared his throat and fiddled with his own napkin. "I've been busy with work."

"I can imagine."

He caught her gaze and electricity sparked between them before Eli's attention dropped to his food. Heat flared in Sienna's cheeks. Holy moly, she really should've made more of an effort to date after they broke up. She'd tried here and there, but no one had ever captured her attention quite like Eli. He was a difficult man to live up to.

She licked her lips. "I haven't dated much either. Work also keeps me busy."

Why was she telling him this? *Shut up, shut up.*

An awkward silence fell over the kitchen. Sienna busied herself with finishing the last of her sandwich. Then she dusted crumbs off her hands. "Thanks again for cooking. I was more hungry than I thought."

"Like I said, it was no trouble." Eli's expression grew

serious. "I was sorry to hear about your dad's heart attack. Your mom says he's on the mend. Is that true?"

"Yeah. He had surgery last week and spent a few days in the hospital. He got the all-clear to leave today, thank God. But the doctors want him to rest and avoid stress." Guilt soured the taste of the buttery grilled cheese, turning it to dust in her mouth. She'd spoken with her family after being released from jail, and her mother assured her Dad was fine, but Sienna hadn't missed the thread of worry buried in her voice.

Her parents must've been terrified when she was arrested.

She wasn't surprised they called Eli. He'd helped her family before. With Harper's case. Back then, Eli was the Texas Ranger for this area. When Sienna showed him the evidence she'd collected on her sister's murder, he'd listened. Followed up. Investigated himself and then eventually arrested the man for murder.

Her sister's killer died in prison, but Eli's steadfastness in the wake of police inaction for years had restored Sienna's faith in law enforcement. A friendship formed between them that later deepened to romance.

Until the incident with Dalton.

Sienna's parents didn't know the ins and outs of why the relationship with Eli ended, only that it did. Given the amount of trouble she was in, it made sense her family turned to the one trusted person in law enforcement they knew.

Sienna pushed away her half-eaten soup. Time to rip off this band aid. "Eli..."

"Don't." He gave a quick shake of his head. "I'm here. I'm helping. End of discussion."

"So what? You cook grilled cheese sandwiches and we talk, just like old times. Do you really think we can simply forget about everything that happened between us?" She stared at him incredulously. "You walked out of my life five years ago and never looked back. I called, I sent letters. You never responded."

"Because there was nothing to say. You made your choice."

His irritatingly calm delivery spiked her temper. Eli had always tweaked her tail in a way no one else could, but normally, Sienna remained rational. The lack of sleep and the horrific events of the past day had weakened her ability to keep her voice level.

"My choice? *My choice?*" She pushed away from the table. "Your brother called from jail, begging me to take him to rehab. He'd been sober for almost a year, but the anniversary of your mother's death was too much for him to handle, and he fell back into drugs. Dalton needed help—"

"He needed to face the consequences of his actions." Eli's voice rose to match her intensity. "He stole my car while high and sideswiped an elderly couple on their way home from a church mixer. It was a miracle no one was killed!" His gaze clashed with hers. "I've been cleaning up Dalton's messes for years. Who sent him to rehab the first time?" He jutted a finger at his chest. "Me. I paid his way, gave him a place to live when he got out, helped him find work. I gave him chance after chance. But at some point, it's enough. I'd reached my limit."

Sienna's anger melted, leaving her feeling hollow. She knew the heartbreak addiction had on family members. Her own sister had been a drug user. It'd wreaked havoc on everyone in their household, and there were times her parents had wanted to give up. But they hadn't.

Unfortunately, Harper was murdered before she ever got sober. Losing her older sister affected Sienna in ways she still struggled with today. It had definitely impacted her desire to help Dalton. "You were angry and weren't seeing things clearly—"

"So you went behind my back and bailed him out of jail." There was no forgiveness in Eli's tone or expression. No understanding or a hint of the softness she'd seen a few minutes ago. It'd been replaced with bitterness and anger. "I needed your support and understanding, instead you betrayed my trust. So yes, you made your choice, Sienna, and there was nothing left for us to say."

Tears pricked her eyes. There was so much she needed to say. About her sister. About how Harper's death had destroyed her, and she was simply trying to prevent Eli from ever facing that same pain. But words wouldn't eek past the lump in her throat. What was the point? He wouldn't listen anyway. Eli's mind was made up. She'd been naïve to think a simple discussion would heal the matter.

It was better he'd never answered her phone calls or letters.

Sienna held back her tears by sheer force of will, taking her empty bowl to the sink and dumping it inside. The spoon clattered against the porcelain. In the window's reflection, Eli's head dropped to his hands. His shoulders rose and fell as he took a deep breath. The silence stretched out.

"What happened between us is in the past," Eli finally said. "I suggest we don't talk about it again. Our focus needs to be on the murder charges against you."

"I don't understand." She turned to face him. "Why are you here? Why help me?"

He dropped his hands and met her gaze. His eyes were the color of a winter sky, but there was nothing cold buried in their depths. It was all heat. Purpose. Strength. But when he spoke, his voice was flat. "Because I took an oath to uphold the law. You're innocent, which means there's a killer running around town. I intend to make sure whoever is responsible ends up behind bars."

It wasn't a declaration of love, or an apology, or even a promise to heal their wounded hearts. It was better. An oath to follow through on his commitment to the badge, something Sienna knew Eli would never betray. He wouldn't stop until the killer was caught.

She'd be a fool to turn him away.

"Okay, but we do this together. As a team. I won't be locked out of my own investigation." She arched a brow. "I need your word, Eli."

He hesitated, his gaze scanning her face, as potent as a touch. Then he gave a sharp nod. "You have it."

That would have to do. Sienna sucked in a deep

breath and let it out slowly. "Let's get started. We only have a little while before my family arrives. They're stopping by once my dad's discharge paperwork is signed by the doctor at the hospital—"

The sound of shattering glass erupted behind her. Sienna ducked just as something whizzed over her head and slammed into the fridge. The scent of gasoline assaulted her nose, seconds before a blaze of fiery heat erupted. Sienna instinctively recoiled, sending her arms up to protect her head, but pain instantly shot through her forearm. Sparks flickered on her sweater sleeve.

She was on fire.

FOUR

Eli had seconds to act.

Grabbing the thick potholder from the counter, he rapidly smothered the sparks threatening to spread up Sienna's sleeve. The fire alarm blared as thick smoke filled the kitchen. It burned his eyes and nose with the horrible stench of burning fuel. But nothing created more panic than the idea of Sienna hurt. Running from the fire would only cause the sparks on her clothes to spread. The first priority had to be her safety.

"I'm okay." Sienna yanked off the sweater, revealing a tank top underneath. Her arm was angry and red, but the burn appeared minor compared to what could've happened. The homemade incendiary device had been chucked straight at her. If she hadn't ducked...

Eli didn't want to think about what would've happened. Instead his gaze swept the kitchen. The blaze was burning along the base of the fridge and the tile floor, but it could be stopped before the entire house was destroyed. "Do you have a fire extinguisher?"

Movement beyond the kitchen window indicated the assailant wasn't done yet.

"Get down!" Eli yanked Sienna behind the kitchen island as another bottle filled with gas flew in through the broken window. This one smashed against the wooden cabinets. A whoosh of heat and flames singed the hair at the base of his neck. Forget about saving the house. They needed to get out.

Sienna must've come to the same conclusion because she grabbed his hand and pulled him toward the living room. Another window exploded in a shower of glass, followed by the couch erupting in a fit of flames. The heat and smoke turned blinding.

Eli dropped to his hands and knees for fresh oxygen, tugging Sienna down with him. He took the lead, hurrying to the front door as another window shattered in the dining room. Several fire alarms in the house blared. Hopefully, one of the neighbors heard the commotion, saw the flames, and called 911.

Sienna grabbed his arm. "We can't go out the front door." She screamed to be heard over the alarms. "He's expecting that."

She was right. The attacker could throw one of his fire bombs at them. Eli was armed, but a handgun was no match for a grenade of gasoline and flames. Whoever was behind this wasn't interested in sparing their lives. He was out for blood. Sienna's blood.

"Climbing out a window is a bigger risk. It'll take too long and give him the opening he's looking for." Eli pulled his handgun. "The front door is our best option."

"No! Follow me." Sienna rose to a crouch and took off down the hallway.

Eli quickly followed, holding his gun in a sweaty grip. His lungs ached with smoke inhalation and his head was woozy from the stench of gasoline. Pain spreading across his abdomen was a fierce reminder that the gunshots he'd incurred a few months ago still affected him physically. Cooler air washed over his heated skin as they entered a rear bedroom.

An office space. Papers piled high in stacks surrounding a laptop. Coffee mugs littered the desk and the credenza, holding court with family photographs and an odd assortment of multicolored files and books. Pens tangled with paper clips and earbuds. Several boxes were scattered on the carpet. The leather chair behind the desk was cracked and worn.

Attached to the office was a waiting room for clients. A leather couch sat opposite a coffee table with ancient magazines. The entire space resembled the rest of the house. Messy and chaotic, no clear organization other than whatever system Sienna had in her mind for the day.

It was baffling to Eli. He was as rigid in his organization as he was in his values. How Sienna managed to solve any case—let alone run circles around the Sandalwood Police Department—while her office resembled something left in the wake of a tornado was beyond him.

She grabbed her laptop and a stack of files, jerking her chin toward the waiting room. "There's another entrance clients use. Through there."

Eli's long strides ate up the distance to the second entrance. He peeked through the shade into a side yard with a walkway. The yellow glow of the streetlights illuminated the space. There was no sign of their attacker. That didn't mean much though. He could be hiding in the shadows behind the garage, lying in wait. It'd been a while since the last Molotov cocktail was thrown inside.

Should they stay in place until the police showed up? It was an option. But not a good one. Smoke was already filling the space and the heat of the flames intensified by the second. They wouldn't last long holed up in the office. Besides, the longer they stayed put, the greater the chance their attacker would figure out there was a second exit. Hopefully, he was still camped out at the front door.

Eli cracked open the door. He peered into the yard and listened for any unnatural sound. Thunder rumbled in the distance as an approaching storm closed in. The air was heavy with the scent of rain and the stink of smoke. Woods bordered this side of the property. A perfect hiding place, provided they could make it there before the attacker struck.

He glanced over his shoulder. Sienna was still frantically gathering papers from her desk. "Let's go."

She didn't pay him any mind. Soot covered her pretty face, and her curls had jettisoned from the ponytail she'd wrangled them into after her shower. Sweat poured off

Eli's face as he closed the distance between them. Flames licked at the entrance of the office. They needed to move.

He snagged her elbow with a gentle hand, but his tone brooked no argument. "Now, Sienna."

She allowed him to drag her to the door. Eli spared another moment to scan the yard again. No movement. Heart pounding, he lifted his weapon and held it at the ready before stepping onto the small porch. Crisp air cooled the sweat on his brow and raised goosebumps along the back of his neck. Leaves on the nearby oak tree rustled.

The attacker was out there. Somewhere. Eli could sense him.

A fear unlike anything Eli had ever known gripped him. He'd been in dangerous situations before. Been shot in the line of duty and had the scars to prove it. But this situation was different. It wasn't a nameless civilian he was protecting, nor was it a fellow member of law enforcement. This was Sienna. *Sienna.* And for some reason he didn't want to examine, it made all the difference.

Indecision once again warred within him, but the sound of the roof creaking inside the house reaffirmed his original choice.

With one hand, he gestured for Sienna to step outside. She did, and he quickly pushed her in front of him. "Head for the tree line."

His voice was barely above a whisper, but she gave a sharp nod. Clutching the laptop and files, she bolted across the yard. Eli followed, keeping his body in line with hers to provide cover, his gaze never resting in one position, his senses heightened for any sign of danger.

A shadow shifted. It moved at a rapid pace away from the garage straight for Sienna.

A man dressed in black, wearing a ski mask.

Holding a flaming bottle in one hand.

FIVE

Sienna's heart pounded against her rib cage as the masked man with the flaming bottle rounded the curve of the garage, heading straight for her. She was unarmed. Outrunning him was possible, but unlikely if his aim was accurate.

"Police!" Eli pointed his weapon, moving directly into Sienna's path, blocking the masked man from getting to her. "Freeze!"

The intruder drew up short. He tossed the flaming bottle in their direction, but it landed short of its intended target, smashing into the ground. A flash of heat followed as the gasoline ignited. Sienna clutched her laptop and the files she'd managed to rescue from her office against her chest like a shield. Behind her, the blaze of the house fire illuminated the night well enough to see the masked man turn tail and run.

Eli took a step forward in pursuit and then halted.

She didn't hesitate. Sienna took off after the intruder,

intent on stopping him before he escaped. Within seconds, Eli was at her side. They rounded the corner in time to hear an engine roar.

"Stop!" Eli shouted.

It was too late. Tires squealed as the assailant took off on a dirt bike down the street and out of sight.

Eli splashed water on his face before wiping at the soot with several paper towels. The last few hours had been spent giving a statement to responding police officers. Then he'd argued with the emergency room doctor about being allowed to stay with Sienna while she received treatment for smoke inhalation and the burn on her arm. An argument he'd won. After the attack, there was no way he was leaving her side for any reason.

He exited the bathroom. Sienna lay on the bed. Her complexion was pale, nearly as white as the sheets, her lips flattened into a thin line. An IV delivered fluids and equipment monitored her heart rate and oxygen levels. The mask that was supposed to be over her nose and mouth had been tossed to the side.

Eli closed the distance between them and picked it up. "Put this on." He scowled. "You need the extra oxygen to help your lungs."

The stubborn woman pushed his hand away and hit the button to shift the bed into a sitting position. Her burned arm was bandaged. "I feel much better. Besides, you and I need to talk about the case. About Albert."

"We can do it later—"

She captured his hand. "No, Eli. We need to do it now. I've been arrested and nearly killed in the span of twenty-four hours. Things are escalating. Someone is desperately trying to prevent me from finding Ruby Morales. If something happens to me, I need you to continue looking for her."

It was on the tip of his tongue to say that nothing was going to happen to her, but Eli bit back the words. That wasn't a guarantee he could make. Instead, he said, "In order for anyone to hurt you, they'll have to go through me. And I don't plan on making it easy."

The corners of her mouth quirked up. "I know, but I'll feel a lot better once we talk." She released his hand and pointed to the stack of papers and the laptop saved from the fire. "Can you grab those for me?"

He did as she asked. Sienna fished a photograph from one of the file folders and handed it to him. The young woman in the picture had a high-forehead covered with side bangs and deep-set brown eyes. Her cheeks were rosy with youth, a crooked tooth gave her smile character, and a cross necklace was nestled in the hollow between her collarbones.

"Ruby is twenty-two." Sienna's voice was hoarse from the smoke inhalation. "Her parents passed away in a car crash when she was five, so she was raised by her maternal grandmother. Ruby works as an administrative assistant for a local charity and was enrolled in online college classes to obtain her master's in business. Three weeks ago, right after New Year's, Ruby met up with some friends at Lone Star Saloon, a local bar. She left around midnight. Alone. Never made it home."

"Had she been drinking?"

"Nope. According to the bartender and her friends, Ruby didn't have anything other than a Diet Coke and water. She's not much of a partier. The initial investigation run by Chief Ramirez didn't yield any significant leads. Her last text was to her grandmother saying she was on her way home. It was sent as she left the bar. Shortly after that, her cell phone stopped transmitting to the towers, as though it'd been turned off. Her car hasn't been found, and no one has heard from her." Sienna leaned against the pillow. "I think something happened when she got to her car that night. The bar doesn't have cameras in the parking lot. Just over the entrance."

Eli surmised where Sienna was headed with the story. "You believe someone kidnapped her?"

"I think it's the most likely scenario. Chief Ramirez believes Ruby simply ran off and she'll pop back up in a few months when she runs out of cash."

"Any reason to believe that?"

"Ruby's debit card has been used in different locations throughout the state. But when footage was pulled from the ATMs, the person who withdrew the money placed a hand over the camera. There's not a clear shot of the person's face."

She pulled out another photograph and handed it to Eli. It was a still taken from an ATM video camera. The person had a hoodie pulled up for concealment and the darkness of the surroundings made it hard to distinguish features. "This does look like a woman."

"I know. The person is about the right height, but Ruby's not the kind of girl who'd simply leave town on a whim. She's responsible. Never missed a day of work or school. Plus, Ruby's dedicated to her grandmother. I find it hard to believe she'd take off without a word to the woman who raised her." Sienna smoothed out an invisible wrinkle from her sheet. "There's one more thing. Two weeks after Ruby disappeared, her grandmother, Amelia, received a phone call from an unknown cell phone. It was Ruby. She begged for help and then whispered something Amelia couldn't make out before hanging up."

"Did Amelia report the phone call to the police?"

Sienna nodded. "Chief Ramirez traced the cell phone number Ruby used to make the call, but it belongs to a burner phone. The last known cell tower the phone pinged was in Sandalwood, near the marina. My informant in the police department says they're monitoring the cell, but it hasn't been turned back on again. I suspect Ruby is being held against her will, somehow got ahold of a cell phone, and made a desperate call to her grandmother. But her kidnapper must've figured out what she did and dumped the phone."

"How does Albert tie into this?"

"Good question. In my initial questioning of family and friends, I discovered Ruby had been on a few dates with a man named Dallas Redding. She decided they weren't a good match and told him so. Dallas wasn't happy with Ruby's rejection and kept hounding her. Texting, calling, showing up while she ran errands in town."

Eli's jaw clenched. "Sounds like stalking to me."

"Me too. Dallas lives on a houseboat in the marina. The same location Ruby made that secret phone call from. I've trailed him a couple of times but haven't uncovered anything suspicious."

"Did you question him?"

"No. I was still gathering intel and didn't want to alert Dallas that I was on to him, in case he decided to kill Ruby."

Smart. Sienna's thoughts were always centered on the victim. There had been other cases where the kidnapper killed his victim in the hopes of avoiding detection. Since Dallas owned a boat, it wouldn't be difficult to dump Ruby's body somewhere in the ocean. She might never be found.

"Albert must've heard I was asking questions because he called my office and asked to meet on his boat," Sienna continued. "He claimed to have important information about Ruby's disappearance. I was hoping he'd seen something that would tie Dallas to the crime. But when I arrived on Albert's boat..." She winced. "Whoever killed him knew I was coming. They broke into my car and stole my weapon while I was at the hospital visiting my dad hours before I was set to meet Albert."

Hospitals were gun-free zones. Eli was allowed to keep his weapon because he was an officer of the law, but Sienna, as a private investigator, didn't have that leverage.

Which is why her gun was locked in her vehicle. He perched on the edge of her bed. "You reported the gun missing to the police, right?"

"Immediately. But Chief Ramirez believes it was a setup. That I planned to kill Albert, so I reported my gun stolen in order to make it look like someone else had done it." She rolled her eyes. "Which is just stupid. Why would I kill Albert and then hang around the boat waiting for the police to show up? Or worse, point my gun at them? I explained to the police chief that I thought it was Albert's killer moving around on the boat, but he didn't believe me."

"There was an anonymous phone call to 911 from a man who reported hearing gunshots at 12:03. What time did you arrive at the marina?"

"Around that time. Maybe a minute or two earlier." She swallowed hard. "I had the sense someone was watching me, but at the time, dismissed it as nerves. Albert was a sketchy character, and I didn't trust him. There were rumors he'd blackmailed people in the past and he'd hinted on the phone that he wanted payment for the information. That's why I had several hundred dollars in cash on me."

Eli mulled over everything she'd told him and a scenario formed in his mind. "Let's assume for a moment Albert had valid information. If that's so, he might've gone to the person who kidnapped Ruby and demanded to be paid for his silence, but was refused. Albert then calls you to add pressure to the person."

"That person decides to kill Albert instead and frame me for the murder. Two birds, one stone."

Eli nodded. "You have the reputation of closing cases. Of not giving up. Seems your investigation into Ruby's disappearance rattled someone's cage."

Sienna opened her mouth to reply, but a knock at the door cut her off. Eli rose from the bed and turned just as Chief Boone Ramirez stepped into the room. From the grim look on the lawman's face, whatever he came to say wasn't good.

Eli stiffened and braced himself for what was coming.

SIX

"We haven't found the arsonist."

Sienna eyed the lawman standing at the end of her hospital bed. Police Chief Boone Ramirez was pushing fifty, but had the craggy look of a man who'd seen too much for his years. Lines crisscrossed his forehead, exacerbated by a retreating hairline and heavily hooded eyes. His uniform was wrinkled, as if he'd tossed on yesterday's clothes after being roused from bed. One hand clutched a takeaway coffee cup, the other, his cell phone.

"Did your officers do a canvass of the neighbors?" Sienna winced as pain lanced her throat, slicing straight through to her lungs. Eli cast her a concerned look. His solid presence was comforting, especially after being hunted by a masked man holding a flaming bottle of gasoline. Sienna didn't consider herself a coward by any means, but the incident at her home had shaken her.

She swallowed and continued past the pain in her throat. "Someone may have seen the motorbike leaving the neighborhood. Or better yet, some of my neighbors could have security cameras. In fact, the Douglas family at the end of the block do."

The chief scowled. "I don't need instructions on how to do my job."

Frustration stiffened her muscles. Chief Ramirez and Sienna didn't have a good relationship, mostly because he was too prideful to admit that mistakes made by his department often meant cases went unsolved. Like her sister's. Sienna's success at finding Harper's killer, and the subsequent decision to ask the Texas Rangers for help, had kicked off a feud between her and the chief that extended to this day. One Boone refused to let go of.

It was a shame. They could work together, trading information as Sienna uncovered it. Instead, the chief saw her as an interloper, someone interested in upstaging and embarrassing him. But she wasn't. Sienna only cared about providing answers to desperate families.

"No one is telling you how to do your job, Chief Ramirez." Eli placed a comforting hand on Sienna's shoulder and squeezed gently. "Sienna's simply asking questions. Honestly, I'm just as interested in the answer."

Boone grunted and turned his glower on Eli. The two men had once worked well together, but assisting Sienna with her sister's case had caused friction between them. Friction that was obviously still there.

"Officers conducted an initial canvass," the chief said. "But didn't come up with anything of interest. If there's time, I'll have more officers knock on doors in the morning."

Sienna's frustration grew. Gathering evidence was a painstaking process, but she sensed Chief Ramirez was slow-walking his efforts. The arsonist had burned down her house and tried to kill her. Surely that deserved more urgency than an "initial" canvass. She pursed her lips. "Whoever was behind the attack is connected to Ruby's disappearance."

The chief grunted. "Is that so?"

"Yes. First Albert is murdered, and then I'm nearly killed hours after making bail. That can't be a coincidence. Ruby's abductor will do whatever is necessary to keep me from working her case."

"Hold on." Chief Ramirez rocked back on the heels of his alligator skin cowboy boots. "Y'all are jumping to some pretty outlandish conclusions. While I agree the attack on Sienna is probably connected to Albert's murder, I doubt it has anything to do with Ruby's disappearance."

"Why is that?" Eli asked.

"Because Albert has a set of cousins. Troublemakers, known for breaking the law and taking matters into their own hands. The Greers have a mafia-style mentality. Come after one and you deal with them all." Boone pegged Sienna with a dark look. "You kicked up a hornet's nest by killing Albert. His family is out for revenge."

She leaned forward in the hospital bed, shaking off Eli's comforting hand, and infused her voice with conviction. "I didn't kill Albert."

Boone merely shrugged. "You're innocent until

proven guilty under the law, but the Greer clan isn't known for being patient."

His expression held no sympathy. Sienna was an alleged killer, but in the chief's mind, she was already guilty as charged. It was one of the many reasons they didn't get along. Investigations required a certain flexibility as new evidence was discovered. Unfortunately, once Chief Ramirez decided on a theory, it was impossible to convince him otherwise.

"I've got officers looking for Albert's cousins," the chief continued. "But Tony and Luis aren't easy to find on the best day. Given the circumstances, I'm sure they've gone underground. We'll question the rest of the family, of course, but they won't be much help."

Sienna's stomach churned with uncertainty. Could the chief be right? Could Albert's cousins be responsible for the attack against her? It was possible. She'd heard rumors about the Greer family. They were known for sticking together, although she hadn't realized that included killing for one another.

The chief's cell phone buzzed with a notification. He glanced at the screen before focusing back on Eli and Sienna. "If I were you, I'd keep a low profile until the trial."

Sienna didn't bother to respond. She had no intention of doing any such thing. Not while Ruby was still missing.

"Chief, the Texas Rangers are available to assist with this investigation." Eli's tone was respectful, but Sienna knew him well enough to catch the faint curve of irritation riding his lip. He didn't like Boone any more than she did. "Your theory about the attack on Sienna could be correct. This may simply be Albert's family seeking revenge, but it's also possible the three cases—Ruby's disappearance, Albert's murder, and this attack on Sienna—are connected. We should let the evidence guide the investigation."

Boone smirked. "There's no need to get the Texas Rangers involved. I've got things well in hand." He tilted his head. "I know you, Eli, and I'm warning you now to be careful. You're on medical leave. Even if you weren't, you don't have the jurisdiction to investigate these cases without my permission. Stand down and stay clear. I'd hate for you to lose your job over this matter."

Sienna inhaled sharply. She sensed rather than saw Eli's muscles stiffen with anger, but his expression remained placid. It was deceptive. A storm brewed underneath that easygoing facade, one that shouldn't be underestimated.

Eli held the chief's gaze. "Don't worry about me, Chief Ramirez. I'm well aware of my responsibilities."

"Good. I'll keep y'all informed of any progress."

With those final words, the chief turned on his heel and left the room. Sienna closed her eyes, sagging against the hospital bed, weariness stealing the last of the strength from her muscles. Ruby was missing. Albert was dead. Someone was trying to kill her. And now Eli's job was on the line if he continued to help. Everything about this case had just become a lot more complicated.

A strong hand brushed curls away from her forehead

and then Eli gently tugged the oxygen mask back over her face. Sienna opened her eyes. Her chest clenched at the tenderness in his expression.

"Don't worry. We're going to figure everything out."

She caught his hand. "We can't. I need to do this on my own, Eli. You heard the chief—"

"Not a chance, Sienna. We're a team, remember?" He smiled, the faint dimple in his cheek appearing. Soot was smeared along his hairline, evidence of the near-death experience they'd been through only hours ago. "You're stuck with me for the time being. Where you go, I go."

She wanted to argue. Knew that she should. But Sienna didn't have any fight left in her. Truth was, deep down, she was scared and there was no one she trusted more to watch her back than Eli. Even after everything they'd been through, she knew with every fiber of her being that he wouldn't let anyone harm her.

Their gazes met, and for a moment, time stopped. Sienna was temporarily overcome with the desire to close the distance between them and sink into Eli's embrace. His arms had always been a safe place.

Sheer willpower held her back. It was one thing to have Eli in her corner. It was quite another to reignite their ill-advised romance. Too much pain, too much hurt, and too many unresolved issues lingered between them.

Sienna released his hand, settling back against the bed. "Neither of us has anywhere to go now that my house burned down. There's a few hotels in Sandal-wood, but that's the first place the killer will look for me, right after my parents' farm. Obviously we can't go there—"

"Nonsense." A booming voice came from the doorway. "The farm is exactly where you're going, little girl."

Eli backed away just as Sienna's father entered the hospital room. Wyatt Evans was fresh off heart surgery, but no one would ever suspect the man had been dangerously close to dying last week. His tall and proud stature was unchanged, his thick hair damp from a shower and curly at the collar. He was dressed in church clothes: corduroys and a button-down.

Wyatt crossed the room and quickly embraced Sienna. She sank into her father's hug, unbidden tears flooding her eyes as the familiar scents of tobacco and pine surrounded her. She turned thirty next month, but no matter how old she got, her dad's presence instantly made her feel cared for.

Sienna swiped at the tears on her cheeks as her mother swooped in on the other side to join the embrace. Leila prided herself on doing whatever was necessary for her family's well-being, from cooking balanced meals to driving a tractor in the field. Her silvery hair was cut in a short bob that was practical and easy. Exhaustion from long nights spent in the hospital at her husband's side had deepened the lines on her face, but nothing could remove the warmth in her expression as she kissed Sienna's forehead. "Your father is right. Your place is on the farm."

"But—"

"No buts, little girl." Wyatt's tone was firm. "Whatever trouble you're in, we'll get through it together."

Landon, Sienna's younger brother, tugged on her foot covered by the sheet. His hair was cropped close to his scalp and his skin tanned from hours spent outside. He grinned. "Don't bother arguing, sis. It won't do any good." He lifted a shoulder. "Besides, the old folks are right."

Wyatt lightly punched his son's shoulder. "Watch who you're calling old."

Sienna laughed as her brother rolled his eyes. Her family had been through a lot with Harper's death, but the tragedy had driven them closer. It was comforting to think of going home, but her father's recent heart attack wasn't something she could ignore. The mirth slid from her expression as she focused on her dad. "The doctors ordered you to rest and relax."

"Sienna Marie Evans, do you think I'll get a wink of sleep if you're not under my roof?" He crossed his arms over his broad chest. "And your mother will be up all night pacing a groove in the floorboards, worrying herself sick. Now no more arguments. The matter is settled." He glanced at Eli and paused before extending his hand. "The police chief explained what you did for Sienna tonight. Thank you."

"No thanks necessary, sir. Although, I wouldn't say no to a spare bed, if one's available where the farm hands sleep. I'd like to stick close to Sienna."

"I'll do you one better. You can have the guest room in our house."

A momentary panic fluttered in Sienna's chest as she suddenly realized how close Eli would be. Sleeping down the hall, working together during the day, eating meals at the same table. There wouldn't be a break. Sienna wanted to believe her heart could withstand it. But after the way Eli rescued her from a killer... the tender way he'd brushed the hair from her forehead...

Now she wasn't so sure.

SEVEN

The Evans farm was nestled in a beautiful swath of land on the outskirts of Sandalwood. Greenhouses lined the left side of the property. A barn was protected by an orchard of pecan trees. Horses grazed in a back pasture. To the right, land stretched out far and wide toward the horizon. In the fall, it would be high with corn crops, but now the fields were desolate. Soon tilling would begin for spring planting.

Eli leaned against the porch railing, morning sunshine warming his shoulders as he guzzled coffee. He'd been up every few hours to patrol the property throughout the night. Fortunately, there'd been no sign of Sienna's attacker. The lack of sleep and the soreness in his body from escaping the fire was catching up to him though. It'd been easy in his twenties to work long hours on barely any shut-eye. Hitting thirty-five had changed matters.

He felt old. Jaded. And weary. It didn't help that he was standing several feet away from his friend and colleague, Texas Ranger Cole Donnelly. Twenty-eight and full of endless energy, Cole was the newest member of Company A. He'd joined their team last May after working as a detective for the Criminal Investigation Division of the state police for six years. Eli had taken the younger man under his wing and a solid friendship had formed as a result. They differed in their approach to cases—Eli was rigid, relying on his training to guide him, whereas Cole was more flexible and analytical—but they both shared a deep commitment to truth and justice.

Cole extended a set of photographs toward Eli. "Meet Luis and Tony Greer. Albert's delinquent cousins."

Eli set his coffee mug down on the railing and took the mug shots. Luis was older by several years, his face square like a Lego man, eyes small and hard. Tony shared his brother's crooked nose and bushy brows, but he maintained some semblance of his youth in rounded cheeks and a soft jawline.

"Their rap sheets are as long as my arm." Cole untwisted the cap on a bottle of water. "Petty stuff in their youth, like stealing cars for joyriding, but in recent years, they've upgraded to illegal drug distribution. I've been investigating them for some time in connection with a surge of opioids in this area, but haven't gotten enough evidence to make a case yet."

"Are you sure they're involved?"

"Yep. I've had a few witnesses tell me as much. Unfortunately, those witnesses are drug users. The State's attorney won't take their word for it without more evidence. I've had Luis and Tony tailed by state troopers, we've searched their homes, and brought them in for questioning. Our efforts haven't yielded anything solid though." Cole's expression darkened. "I've also had witnesses disappear. Drug users are notorious for taking off, but it's happened enough times I suspect Luis and Tony are taking matters into their own hands. Not that I can prove it."

Eli frowned. "What do you know about Luis and Tony's relationship with their cousin?"

"Albert kept his nose clean, for the most part, but the family is tight. Long story short, Chief Ramirez is right. Either Luis or Tony could be the man responsible for the attack on Sienna last night. I know you only saw one assailant, but it's still possible the brothers are working together."

Eli nodded, his gaze drifting over the property. Sienna's parents had left early in the morning for follow-up doctor appointments. Her brother, Landon, was working on an old truck near the barn. A Labrador slept peacefully in the grass nearby.

It was terrifying to think that two criminals might do something to harm this family in order to get to Sienna. He prayed for God's help in protecting them. "Chief Ramirez was certain Luis and Tony would do what was necessary to get revenge and would go underground afterward until the dust settled."

"I agree with him. These boys are criminals, but they aren't stupid." Cole studied him for a moment. "How much has Sienna shared with you about what happened on the night Albert was murdered?"

"Everything." Eli quickly went through what Sienna had told him. "The evidence supports her version of events. It's something Chief Ramirez should take seriously, but he won't. He's made up his mind that she's guilty."

"Is there a chance he's right?" Cole lifted up his hands in the classic sign of surrender. "Don't bite my head off. I wouldn't be a friend if I didn't ask. Sienna doesn't have the best reputation with law enforcement in these parts. She's been known to push boundaries and omit pieces of the story to get what she wants. I understand there's history between you two, and admittedly I don't know the full story, but I'd hate for you to invest in someone who isn't telling you the whole truth."

An irrational anger sparked heat in Eli's chest as his protective instincts flared. He met Cole's gaze dead on. "Sienna is innocent. End of story." He lifted the mug shots. "Thanks for the update. And for talking to the chief. I'll take it from here."

Cole opened his mouth and then closed it before seeming to wrestle with his words. Then he sighed. "I have to say this. Tread lightly, Eli. Chief Ramirez can't fire you, but a complaint lodged with Lieutenant Rodriguez will have to be taken seriously. It could mean a sanction, or depending on the offense, something worse."

The warning was fair. Their boss, Lieutenant Vikki

Rodriguez, was a straight shooter who ran Company A by the book. She gave grace when appropriate but didn't suffer fools. If the chief filed a complaint alleging that Eli was interfering with a police investigation, he'd end up in a lot of hot water. He could even be fired.

It was a risk he would have to take. Based on the conversation with Chief Ramirez yesterday, Sienna wasn't going to get a fair shake with the police department. Eli couldn't stand by and do nothing.

The creak of the screen door preceded Sienna's light footsteps as she came onto the porch. The wind rustled her curls, flipping a few across the sweet curve of her cheek. She was dressed in tight jeans and an oversized sweater the color of a ripe plum. In each hand, she held a mug. "Morning. I saw you guys out here and thought you might want some coffee."

Her gaze met Eli's briefly, causing his heart to skip a beat. Irritation followed. Cole's warning wasn't far off the mark. Sienna was his own special weakness, and he hated this hum of attraction shimmering below the surface between them. It was distracting. Sienna wasn't a killer— he'd bet his badge on that—but that didn't mean Eli trusted her completely. Not after what happened with Dalton.

Sienna's attention shifted to Cole. Her gaze seemed to assess him in one swoop while simultaneously gauging the tension levels. How much of their conversation had she overheard? Eli was willing to bet at least some of it.

She forced a polite smile. "I'm Sienna."

"Texas Ranger Cole Donnelly." He tipped his cowboy hat in her direction. "Appreciate the coffee, ma'am, but I've got to run." He turned to Eli. "Call if you need anything."

"Will do. Thanks."

Cole hightailed it to his truck and did a three-point turn before heading down the driveway toward the country lane leading back to town.

Sienna stepped closer, extending one of the mugs toward Eli. "He doesn't like me much."

"He doesn't know you."

She arched a brow. "He thinks I'm a killer, and based on his warning to you about your job, thinks you're foolish to be hitching your wagon to mine."

Sienna leaned against the porch pillar, close enough Eli could smell her distracting perfume. Apples and sunshine. He caught himself before taking a deep breath.

"How much does he know about us?" she asked.

"Only that we were engaged and things ended." He shrugged. "I didn't tell anyone about what happened between us. Not even Ryker. It was..." Too painful to discuss. Heat churned in Eli's belly as the memory of Sienna's betrayal threatened to raise his blood pressure all over again. He tightened his hand on the coffee mug. "Cole is protective, that's all. Company A is a tight-knit group and we watch out for each other."

"Don't worry. I'm not offended." She tucked a loose curl behind her ear. "You deserve to have friends who'll protect you."

So why didn't you? The question was on the tip of his tongue, but he swallowed it back down. Restarting that conversation would only end in heartbreak. Instead, Eli handed her the mug shots. "Cole agrees that Luis and Tony Greer could be responsible for the attack last night."

Sienna frowned. "Is there any evidence directly linking them to the attack?"

"No, but since Chief Ramirez is tackling this angle, I suggest we focus on searching for Ruby Morales. Albert's murder is likely connected to her disappearance. Locating Ruby will hopefully lead us to the killer."

Her shoulders sagged with apparent relief. "There's nothing I'd like more than to find Ruby. I keep praying she's alive, but I'm worried that's not the case."

Eli feared she was right. If someone murdered Albert to ensure his silence, then chances were Ruby had also been killed. "I did a background check on Dallas Redding, your primary suspect in Ruby's disappearance. He's never been arrested, but two of his exes took restraining orders out against him. Considering he lives at the marina and could've slipped onto Albert's boat to kill him before your arrival the other night, he's the first person we need to talk to."

"You know he's not going to tell you the truth about where he was on the night Ruby disappeared. Or when Albert was killed." She hesitated. "And what if Ruby is alive, and he's holding her? Won't questioning Dallas tip him off?"

Eli arched his brows. "Not if we make a show of interviewing everyone at the marina."

A slow smile stretched across Sienna's face. "Nice cover." She hurried back to the house. "I'll grab my coat. You drive."

EIGHT

"Some things never change."

Eli glanced at Sienna. She ran a finger over the dash of his truck and then lifted it into the sunlight. "Not a speck of dust." Her lips curved up into a smile. "Do you still clean the inside every day?"

He shifted in his seat. "Not every day. This is my personal vehicle, so there are days it doesn't move from my driveway." Eli used an official state vehicle for work. He didn't mention that was also ruthlessly scrubbed regularly. Nothing made him feel more out of control than an untidy space. "Cleanliness is close to godliness." He shot her a smile. "I vaguely remember your mother agreeing with that sentiment."

That comment earned him a laugh. It was light. Joyful. Eli was struck with the notion that he'd missed Sienna's laugh almost as much as he'd missed their conversations. Their good-natured debates too. He was tidy, she was messy. Ketchup was necessary with fries, but Sienna insisted on mayonnaise. He was an early riser, she didn't want to talk to anyone before ten.

Their disputes over these issues had always ended in laughter and kisses.

That was a road he didn't want to go down. So before Sienna could launch into a counter-argument, Eli punched the stereo button, letting the sound of country music spill into the cab. He kept his gaze on the road beyond the windshield. Sandalwood hadn't changed much in the intervening years. The small town was comprised of five stop lights and the marina. The winter months were reserved for locals, but in the summer, the population swelled to double or even triple the normal size.

"Did you see the front page of the local newspaper this morning?" Eli focused on the task at hand, steering the conversation back to safe grounds. "The reporter who wrote the article did a deep dive into Albert's murder and the possible connection to Ruby's disappearance. She also insinuated Chief Ramirez was incompetent."

"I had nothing to do with the article, but the reporter is a friend of mine. Her aunt was killed, and the case had gone stone cold until I took it on. The murderer was the ex-husband, and I found enough evidence to prove he was guilty." She sighed. "Chief Ramirez is going to be hopping mad today. It's not the first time he's faced accusations of incompetence. I don't take any pleasure in it, but I also won't apologize for doing my job."

"All the more reason to keep a low profile when we talk to Dallas. Let me lead the conversation."

She glanced at him, and for a moment, Eli thought Sienna would argue, but then she nodded. Minutes later, they pulled into the marina parking lot. Brine scented the air. Sienna gestured to a souped-up Toyota Tacoma on the far side of the lot. "That belongs to Dallas."

Eli's brows raised slightly. He drew closer to the truck, adding up the cost of the oversized tires, custom rims, and the special exhaust pipe. Those upgrades cost several thousand dollars. Interesting spending habits for a man who lived on a boat and offered excursions to tourists during the summer. Eli was tempted to look inside the vehicle, but it required standing on the running board. A step too far for a lawman working outside the boundaries of his jurisdiction.

Sienna had no such qualm. She grabbed a hold of the sideview mirror with one gloved hand and peeked inside the passenger side window. "It's clean inside. Cleaner than your car, Eli, and that's saying something."

He glanced over his shoulder to make sure no one was watching them. The lot was empty.

Sienna peeked in the rear window of the extended cab. "He also has an expensive stereo system and top-of-the-line interior. This is one expensive truck for a man who only works part of the year as a tour guide." She hopped down to the pavement. "No sign of Ruby, although that's not saying much. It looks like the vehicle has been detailed inside. And recently. I can still see vacuum marks on the carpet."

Eli had worked in law enforcement long enough to recognize patterns in individuals. A man willing to stalk and harass former girlfriends was a breath away from escalating to a more dangerous crime. Had Dallas set his sights on Ruby, and when she rejected him, took matters into his own hands? It was a strong possibility.

But was he smart enough to murder Albert and frame Sienna for the crime?

That wasn't as clear. Eli grabbed Sienna's hand and pulled her away from the truck. "We can't jump to conclusions based on the man's vehicle. Vacuuming the inside of your car isn't a crime."

"Obviously. Otherwise, you'd be in jail for life."

He ignored her jab. "I can't see what any of this has to do with Ruby's disappearance. If she was nabbed, it was in her own car. There's no reason for Dallas to use his truck to transport her."

"Don't you think it's weird though? Where did Dallas get the money for the upgrades on his truck? Not to mention his yacht. It's worth at least two hundred thousand."

"Without a deep dive into his finances, there's no way to know if the money he's spending is unreasonable." Since Eli wasn't officially assigned to the case, he couldn't obtain a warrant for those documents. In fact, any background check he conducted was limited to publicly available sources. "He could've inherited the money. Or lived frugally over the years. There are a thousand and one possible reasons why Dallas has the cash to afford both the yacht and his truck."

The next hour was spent questioning individuals at the marina. Most had heard about Ruby's disappearance and the murder of Albert. No one had valuable information to add. Several tried to question Sienna about her role in the crime, but she dodged the questions easily. Eli admired the friendly way she handled the pressure. Her smile and charm put most people at ease.

Boats bobbed in the water and seagulls screamed as they made their way to Dallas's vessel. The forty-foot yacht had a sleek aerodynamic design with a fiberglass hull and teak accents. An outdoor table was sheltered from the sun by a canopy and mirrored sliding doors led to the interior. The gangway was extended, although there was a sign hanging across the ropes showing guests were not welcome.

"Hello?" Eli called out. "Anyone home?"

The mirrored doors swished open and a man emerged. Dallas Redding. Eli immediately recognized him from his company's website. Tall, with a lean build, he was tanned from working outside all year. Dark stubble covered the bottom half of his face and a tattoo peeked out from the collar of his sweater. His gaze swept over Eli and Sienna, but curiosity didn't flicker in the depths. "Sorry, guys, I don't offer tours in the winter."

Eli had the sense Dallas knew who they were and why they were there, but played along. He returned his amiable smile. "We're not here for a tour. My name is Eli Goodwin and this is Sienna Evans. We were hoping to talk to you about Ruby Morales."

"Ruby?" His eyebrows arched. "Are y'all cops?"

Eli had to be careful. He had no legal authority to

work Ruby's disappearance and therefore couldn't use his status as a lawman to gain Dallas's cooperation.

"I was hired by Ruby's grandmother," Sienna said smoothly. "She's worried about her granddaughter, and it's my understanding that you and Ruby knew each other. Any information you can provide would go a long way to helping us find her."

Dallas hesitated and then unhooked the sign to join them on the dock. "I heard Ruby left town of her own accord."

"It's a possibility we're pursuing." Eli noticed the other man didn't invite them onto the boat. It didn't mean Dallas was hiding something, but it seemed odd. "Your yacht is gorgeous. Mind letting us on board? I've always been interested in purchasing something like this for myself."

"Normally, I would, but I'm pressed for time today. Come back next week and I'll be happy to give you the full tour."

Sienna's attention was locked on the mirrored doors leading to the interior cabin. She casually strolled down the dock toward the rear of the boat. Eli kept his gaze locked on Dallas. "When was the last time you saw Ruby?"

"You know, I'm not sure." Dallas pulled a cell phone out of his pocket and shot off a text message. "Sorry. I've got meetings lined up this afternoon with potential business partners. I'm thinking of expanding the tour business." He clicked the phone closed and arranged his features in an expression of concern. "Anyway, Ruby.

She's a real nice girl, but we weren't close. I barely knew her."

"Friends said y'all went on a date or two."

"Yeah." Dallas rubbed the back of his neck, a sheepish look creeping across his features. "But you know how it is, man. Ruby was sweet, but things were casual from my end."

Casual? Not according to her friends. Dallas was stalking Ruby, but accusing him of that would end the conversation quickly. "Were you surprised when she left town?"

"Not really. Ruby talked of taking a road trip. She was tired of being responsible all the time." Dallas dropped his hand. "I think she was inspired by my adventures. I'm a rolling stone. There's nothing better than having the ability to lift the anchor on my boat and escape for a while. I'm sure her grandmother is worried, but I don't think she should be. Ruby will pop back up when she's done exploring."

"I'm sure." Eli kept his stance and tone casual. "Do you remember where you were on the night she disappeared?"

"Actually, I do. I had a cold that day, so I stayed in, which was unusual for me. Friday nights are usually date nights." He flashed a knowing smile. Obviously Dallas wanted to make it clear that he had an exciting dating life. To distance himself from Ruby? Probably.

"Can anyone verify where you were that night? We're asking everyone about their whereabouts. It helps the investigation." Eli rocked back on his heels and let his grin widen. "Maybe you had someone to nurse you back to health?"

"'Fraid not. The one time I like to be alone is when I'm sick."

"Got it. Well, maybe one of your neighbors here in the marina can confirm you were home?"

"I doubt it. There aren't many people who live on their boats like I do. This place is pretty quiet at night." His phone beeped with an incoming text, and Dallas glanced at the screen. "Sorry to cut this short, but I gotta go."

"One more thing," Sienna jumped back into the conversation. "Did you know Albert Greer?"

Dallas frowned, but a flicker of anger flared in his expression before he could erase it. "That fisherman who was shot the other night? I heard about it, but I didn't know the guy personally." He tilted his head. "What does that have to do with Ruby?"

"I can't say, but Albert blackmailed people. Know anything about that?"

His gaze turned hard. "No." He tucked his cell phone back in his pocket and strolled onto the walkway, replacing the sign to keep visitors out. "I hope you locate Ruby soon. I'm sure she'll have lots of adventures to share when you do."

He went back inside the cabin. Eli tilted his head to indicate Sienna should follow him. They strolled out of earshot and then she said, "He's lying. About his relationship with Ruby and about Albert too."

"Agreed." Eli continued down the floating dock. His

stomach churned as an insidious thought formed in his mind. Was Ruby on Dallas's boat? Inside the cabin, tied up and helpless? His hands balled into fists. "Did you see any sign of Ruby?"

"No, but all the windows are mirrored. If she's in there, no one would know unless she came out on deck."

"Where is Albert's boat? I'd like to look at it."

Sienna led him toward the left side of the marina. Albert's fishing boat had seen better days. Rust gathered on the hull and the deck was littered with gear. Crime scene tape cordoned off the entrance.

Eli moved up and down the dock studying his immediate surroundings. "Albert doesn't have a clear view of Dallas's boat from here."

Sienna shrugged. "He could've seen something while walking on the dock. The marina isn't that big, and he'd have to pass by Dallas's boat to get here."

She had a point. Except some of the facts didn't add up. "If Dallas kidnapped Ruby from the bar parking lot and brought her here, what did he do with her car? And how did he get back to his truck without anyone noticing?" Car riding services didn't exist in this rural area. Without a vehicle or a friend with a vehicle, a person was stuck. "Last call is at two in the morning, and Dallas's truck is memorable. Someone—a waitress, a bartender, another patron—would've remembered seeing it in the parking lot."

"I haven't interviewed everyone who worked at the bar." Sienna rubbed her forehead. "I've only had the case a couple of days, and my investigation is in its early stages. I haven't even gone to her workplace yet—"

A roar cut off the rest of her sentence. Eli turned in time to see a speedboat racing across the water at breakneck speed. His heart lurched. The bow of the vessel was pointed at the floating dock, right where Eli and Sienna were standing.

It was going to kill them.

NINE

"Run!"

Eli's order was unnecessary. Sienna had already calculated the trajectory of the speedboat barreling toward them and realized it was on a collision course. She bolted for the safety of the shore, but the driver of the boat deviated to ensure they were in his path.

They couldn't outrun it.

She grabbed Eli's hand and pulled him toward the edge of the dock. Immediately understanding her intentions, and without a word, he interlaced their fingers. The solid strength of his touch provided a comfort she registered instinctively. Their footfalls pounded against the wood as the speedboat roared closer. The water would be freezing, but there was no other option. Without slowing down, and with a silent prayer in her heart, Sienna took a giant leap.

Her hand tore free of Eli's. The cold shocked her lungs. Her boots and jacket dragged her deeper into the murky water. Sienna sank, desperate to put space between her and the oncoming vessel.

Above her head, the water swirled as the speedboat tore through the wood and steel dock, tossing the planks like toothpicks into the water. Vibrations from the collision rippled through her body. Her lungs, damaged from smoke inhalation, burned at the lack of oxygen. She wouldn't be able to stay down much longer. But the engine of the speedboat churned the water, making it cloudy, and Sienna was disoriented.

Which way was up?

She struggled to move her body through the frigid water. Following instinct more than reason, she kicked her legs toward what she hoped was the surface. Her chest screamed for release. For air. She tried to swim faster, but her body couldn't obey the command. Her heart rate roared in her ears. It felt like her chest was about to explode. Any second her body would reflexively take a breath, filling her lungs with ocean water. She'd die.

Please, God, give me strength.

At the last moment, Sienna's head cleared the surface of the water. She dragged in a desperate breath. The relief was short-lived as she spun in a circle. Pieces of the dock floated in the water. The speedboat had crashed into Albert's fishing vessel, but the engine was still running. There was no sign of Eli.

Had he drowned?

Fear gripped Sienna. Her heart thundered against her rib cage as she desperately trod water. Their relationship had ended on a sour note, but not a day had gone by that she hadn't thought of him. Prayed for him and his safety. When Eli was shot last year, it'd driven home the need to make amends, but he hadn't been ready. Maybe she should have pushed. Or done a better job handling their conversation in her kitchen a few nights ago. Would she lose him before getting the chance to make things right?

In the back of her mind, Sienna cursed her stubborn pride. Then she put all her focus on the task at hand. Sucking in another deep breath, she screamed, "Eli!"

There was no answer.

Suddenly, movement on the boat caught her attention. The driver—a man dressed in a ski mask and black clothing—lifted a handgun. He pointed it straight at her. Sienna's gaze locked on the dark barrel. Hypothermia slowed her thinking as her vision narrowed.

Something grabbed Sienna's leg. She instinctively sucked in a breath as a force dragged her under the surface. A bullet whizzed past her head in the water as strong arms embraced her.

Eli.

She gripped his broad shoulders as he pointed in a direction to show where they should go. Sienna nodded, even as her lungs complained again. She tried to get her body to cooperate, but her movements were slow.

More bullets flew through the water above their heads as the assailant continued to shoot at them. Eli gripped her hand, hauling Sienna toward safety.

Finally, he pulled them to the surface.

Sienna inhaled, her abused lungs spasming in reaction. She'd always considered herself physically fit, but these recent attacks showed she needed to spend more time in the gym.

Eli was also winded. He tenderly brushed the hair out of her face, worry punctuating his words. "Are you hurt?"

"No."

Relief creased his features, and then he held a finger up to his lips. They'd surfaced near another fishing vessel. Judging from the way the man on the speedboat was searching the water, he was looking for them. Sienna's body trembled as her exhausted legs tried to keep her above the surface. They couldn't hide here for long. Another few minutes and her body would start shutting down from hypothermia.

"Hey!" a man's voice shouted.

Dallas Redding. He lifted a rifle to his shoulder and said, "Freeze!"

The masked man paid him no mind. He jumped to the steering wheel of the speedboat, and with a horrible grinding sound, pulled away from Albert's fishing vessel. Within seconds, he was racing away.

"Over here!" Eli shouted. He turned to Sienna. "Can you make it to the dock?"

"I think so." She gritted her teeth and forced her muscles to cooperate. The last few feet were too much though.

Eli grabbed Sienna's jacket collar and pulled her along.

Dallas ran to the edge of the broken dock and

lowered his rifle to offer a hand. He pulled Sienna out first before helping Eli. "Are you guys okay? I saw the collision and heard the gunshots. The police are on the way."

Eli answered him, but Sienna didn't register the words. She collapsed against the ground. Her heart thundered in her chest and her teeth chattered. She closed her eyes. If she could sleep for just a moment...

"Don't you dare! Wake up, Sienna." Eli pulled her into a standing position. "Dallas, we need to use your boat."

"Of course. Come on."

Sienna couldn't feel any of her toes. She put one foot in front of the other, Eli's arm around her waist urging her forward even when she wanted to quit. The trembling in her body increased. She couldn't stop her teeth from chattering.

Once they were inside Dallas's yacht, Eli yanked off her jacket and her sweater, leaving her in a tank top and her jeans. He wrapped a thick blanket around her shoulders before sitting her next to a heating vent. Next, he removed her socks and shoes, adding another blanket onto her feet. Dallas left, saying something about flagging down the police when they arrived.

Sienna hugged the blanket around her body. Her eyes drifted closed. The warmth spilling from the vent warmed her numb toes, and feeling returned with a vengeance. Pins and needles assaulted her limbs, and the shivers lessened. Every muscle in her body hurt.

Eli, shirtless, with a blanket tossed over his shoulders,

joined her on the long couch that served as a lounge space. In one hand, he held a towel. He gently began to dry her still dripping hair. "Stay awake for me, Sienna. EMS will be here soon."

His touch was intoxicating. A warmth that had nothing to do with the air flowing from the vent at her feet surged through her veins. Sienna moved closer to him on the couch, her gaze falling to the mottled scars visible on his abdomen. Once again, she was struck by how close Eli had come to being killed last year. And again, just now.

Her hand reached out and pressed against his bare chest. Despite the freezing water temperatures, his skin was warm to the touch. His heart thumped against her palm. Solid. Steady.

A lump formed in her throat. One that couldn't be dislodged as tears filled her eyes. There was so much to say, but her muddled brain couldn't string the words together. This man hadn't been her first love, but he was the one she'd intended to spend the rest of her life with. Losing him had scarred her deeply.

If he'd died in the water... before she'd said her piece... Sienna couldn't have borne that.

She swallowed down the lump in her throat. "Eli..."

He stilled as his gaze lifted to meet hers. Sienna could've drowned in his eyes. They were dark recesses of fathomless blue that reached right inside her chest and grabbed hold of her heart.

Her breath stalled. Suddenly, she became aware of every place they were touching. Eli's hand cupping her cheek, his fingers tangled in her hair, and his thigh pressed up against hers. Desire, a longing that'd existed since the moment she'd seen him standing outside the police department two days ago, urged her closer.

Without a word, Eli tipped his head forward and captured her mouth with his. Heat blasted through every part of Sienna as wisdom and logic and reason fled. There was nothing but emotion. A passion that'd formed the basis for their relationship so long ago, fueled by a connection neither of them could deny. It'd been easy to forget while apart. Simple enough for Sienna to convince herself that what she'd shared with Eli had been better in her head than in real life.

But that was a lie.

Her hand snaked up to wrap around his neck as he deepened the kiss. Molten lava filled her insides as her heart tumbled into the past.

Then abruptly, Eli pulled away.

Cold air rushed in to replace the warmth of his body. Dazed, Sienna blinked as she registered the look of shock on Eli's face. She reached for him, but he backed away.

"That shouldn't have happened. I'm sorry."

"Eli, wait." Her words came out in a rush. "Let's talk. Give me a chance to explain—"

"No." His tone was hard and unyielding, shocking her into silence with its finality. Eli refused to meet her gaze as he gently wrapped the blanket back around her shoulders. "Someone tried to kill you. Again. In order to solve this case, I need to focus. Which means that what-ever happened in the past needs to stay there." He retreated from the couch. "The police must be here. I'll be right back."

He marched to the sliding glass doors without a backward glance. They swished closed behind him, leaving her alone and heartbroken all over again.

Just as she'd feared.

TEN

The Sandalwood Police Department hummed with activity. Eli paced the hallway outside of an interrogation room. Sienna was inside, along with her attorney, Chief Ramirez, and Texas Ranger Cole Donnelly.

It'd been hours since the attack at the marina. Eli had already given his statement, but per protocol, Sienna had to be interviewed separately. Since she was charged with Albert's murder, Isabella Gomez, her attorney, had insisted on being present.

Would the chief finally agree to have the Texas Rangers join the case? Would he realize Sienna was innocent of Albert's murder? Would there be a follow-up investigation into Ruby's disappearance?

Eli prayed the answers to all of those questions would be yes. The attacks on Sienna's life were becoming increasingly violent. Having the Sandalwood Police Department's cooperation could make the perpetrator think twice about trying again. Especially if the Texas Rangers were also involved.

There was no one Eli trusted more than the members of his own team. They'd move heaven and earth to get to the truth.

"Stop pacing." Texas Ranger Ryker Montgomery approached carrying crackers from the vending machine and a set of takeaway coffees. His dark hair was messy, as if he'd run his hands through it dozens of times, and his clothes were wrinkled from the long drive out to Sandal-wood. He jerked his chin toward a chair. "Sit before you work a groove in the floor."

Eli reluctantly claimed the chair. His skin felt itchy from the salt water. He'd been able to change into dry clothes, thanks to the spare set he kept in his truck at all times, but hadn't had a shower. Nor had he eaten since this morning. The sight of the crackers made his stomach rumble. He tore open the package.

Ryker straddled another chair before handing Eli a coffee. "What's got you all worked up?"

"Other than the fact that a maniac in a speedboat tried to kill Sienna?" Eli shoved a cracker in his mouth and chewed furiously before downing it with coffee. The dark brew shot straight through him. He put his thumb and forefinger millimeters from each other. "It was this close, Ryker. If we'd jumped a second or two later, you'd be searching for our bodies in the water."

Ryker wasn't fazed by the last comment. He took a swig of his own coffee. "I highly doubt that's the reason you're in a snit. Don't forget, I was there when you were shot last year. You were totally calm." He leveled his gaze. "So why don't we cut to the chase and you tell me what's really bothering you?"

Eli should've known his best friend would see right through him. The two men had grown up together, and there were few secrets between them.

Except for one.

The real reason Eli and Sienna broke up. He hadn't wanted to discuss it, to explain how badly it hurt when she betrayed him. But given the way he was still reeling from that passionate kiss...

He pinched the bridge of his nose. "It's complicated."

"We've got time. Start talking."

Eli gave Ryker the quick details. The phone call from Dalton asking to be bailed out of jail and his decision not to. "Sienna tried to talk to me, but I shut her down. I was done helping Dalton, and honestly, jail was where he deserved to be after nearly killing that couple in the car accident." Eli's jaw clenched. "Unknown to me, the next morning Dalton called her and begged again to be taken to rehab. She made the unilateral decision to bail him out. I found out about it later that afternoon."

Understanding flashed across Ryker's face. "You felt betrayed."

"Of course. Dalton was my brother. It was my decision, and she should've supported me in it."

"What was Sienna's explanation?"

Eli breathed out. "I never asked. I broke up with her and never looked back. Until she was arrested. I thought..." He rose from the chair, unable to sit still. "I'd get her out of trouble and haul tail back home. Except this case is more complex than I thought. Sienna's life is being threatened."

He hated thinking about the harrowing moments of the last few days. How close Sienna had come to dying. First, the fire at her house and now the speedboat. "When we jumped in the water and she didn't resurface..." His chest tightened. "It was terrifying."

Ryker's expression was sympathetic. He'd had his own frightening experiences protecting a woman in danger. Hannah was now his wife, but before that, she'd nearly died at the hands of a killer. If anyone understood what Eli was going through, it was his best friend.

He sucked in a breath and admitted the rest. "After we got out of the water, when things were safe, I kissed her. Which was a huge mistake. I told Sienna as much." He groaned and collapsed back into the chair. "She's barely looked at me since then. This is a mess. How am I going to prove Sienna's innocence, find Ruby, and stop a killer with all of this personal stuff getting in the way?"

Ryker was quiet for a long moment. "Here's a revolutionary idea. Why don't you clear the air with Sienna? Discuss what happened five years ago."

Eli wasn't sure he wanted to open that can of worms. "I don't think that's a great idea."

"Well, avoiding the conversation isn't working. It's obvious the two of you have unresolved feelings for each other, and those emotions will continue to create a distraction until there's some kind of understanding. My suggestion: if you want to solve this case, hear Sienna out. Give her a chance to explain her side of things."

He tugged on his shirt. "What if that makes things worse?"

"Then you'll deal with it." Ryker lifted his coffee cup and grinned. "You can call and cry on my shoulder."

"Ha ha."

The smile dropped from Ryker's lips. "In all seriousness, you should have given Sienna a chance to explain a long time ago. She wasn't a woman you'd been on one or two dates with. She was your fiancée. Knowing her like I do, she probably has a good reason for bailing Dalton out against your wishes."

Shame prickled Eli as his friend's words sank into him. He'd been so consumed by his righteous anger, he'd refused to hear Sienna out. That wasn't fair.

The door to the interrogation room opened and Chief Ramirez marched out. His expression was stormy. He barely glanced at Eli. Instead, he locked eyes with Ryker. "Ranger Montgomery. My office. Now."

Ryker rose to his feet as Cole emerged. The younger lawman's expression gave nothing away, but he dealt Eli a reassuring nod.

The men disappeared into the chief's office. Through the glass wall, the chief began talking, his face red. Whatever he had to say, it wasn't pleasant.

"He's furious." Sienna joined Eli. Someone—probably her attorney—had brought a dry change of clothes for her. The jeans hugged her curves and the long-sleeve T-shirt highlighted the natural rosiness in her cheeks.

Curls, more defined by the salt water, waved around her heart-shaped face.

Without realizing it, Eli's gaze dropped to her lips. The memory of their passionate kiss flashed in his mind before he could banish it.

Isabella Gomez joined them. Sienna's defense attorney wore a dark red suit with a black blouse underneath. Her hair was tied into an intricate knot. Smart and ambitious, she defended her clients with every legal avenue available to her.

"The only person Chief Ramirez should be furious with is himself." Isabella sniffed. "If he'd investigated Ruby's disappearance properly, this entire mess could've been avoided. Not to mention, Albert might still be alive." Her gaze locked with Eli's. "Ranger Donnelly was receptive to the concept that these cases—Ruby's disappearance, Albert's murder, and the attacks on Sienna—are connected. It seems Luis and Tony Greer haven't been seen by their family in weeks. Houston Police Department issued a warrant for their arrests today in connection with a murder three weeks ago."

Eli rocked back on his heels, his gaze shooting between Isabella and Sienna. "That doesn't eliminate them as suspects in the attacks against Sienna, but it sure sounds like the Greer boys went underground weeks ago."

"Agreed. I don't think they're behind this. Hopefully, the rangers will assist on this case so we can get some answers." Isabella reached into her bag and pulled out a cell phone. She handed the device to Sienna. "Before I forget, here. I had my assistant pick up a new one for you since yours was waterlogged. It's already programmed with your number."

Sienna sighed with relief. "Thank you."

Eli's lips twitched. "You didn't think to pick one up for me, Isabella?"

She shot him a haughty look. Eli wasn't her favorite person—not after breaking up with Sienna. He couldn't blame her for taking his ex's side. But Isabella surprised him by pulling out a new cell phone in a box and extending it in his direction. "Ryker told me what model to get. I hope it's correct. Call your provider and have them port your old number to it, but once that's done, you'll be back in business."

He accepted the box. "Wow. I was joking. I didn't actually expect you to buy me a cell phone."

"You're helping Sienna. It's the least I could do." Her lips softened into a grin. "Besides, I intend to bill you for the phone and my assistant's time."

He laughed. "It's a deal."

Isabella turned to Sienna. "Call me if you need anything else."

"Will do."

The two women hugged and then Isabella left. Sienna rubbed her temple absently with one finger as if she was fighting back a headache. Her complexion was pale, and she looked exhausted.

Eli gently took her elbow and pushed her into a nearby chair before handing her the bag of crackers. "Eat something. You'll feel better."

She tossed him a grateful smile before fishing out a cracker and popping it in her mouth. He offered her his coffee too. Technically they could leave, but Eli wasn't going anywhere until the conversation between the chief and his colleagues was finished. At the moment, Cole was talking. His expression was calm, and the chief seemed to be listening. Progress.

"I didn't see any sign of Ruby in Dallas's boat." Sienna wrapped her hands around the takeaway coffee cup. "Did you?"

"No." Eli took the chair recently abandoned by Ryker. "Initially, when he wouldn't give us a tour, I thought she might be on board. But after the attack, he came to our rescue and didn't hesitate to shelter us inside the cabin."

Sienna frowned, twirling the coffee cup. "Maybe I focused too quickly on Dallas. I think we should look for other suspects." Her movements slowed, her gaze nearly meeting his before skittering away. "I mean... unless you've decided that you're done with this case. I wouldn't blame you." Her words tumbled out in a rush. "You nearly died today too and—"

"I'm not going anywhere." Eli placed his hand on her forearm. The fabric of her shirt was soft under his callused palm.

Nerves jittered his insides at the simple touch. Oh yeah, their earlier kiss had unleashed all his pent-up emotions. Ryker was right. There was no way to move forward without coming to an understanding. "In fact, I think you and I should talk later."

Now her gaze shot up to meet his. Surprise flickered in the multicolored depths. Blues and greens and a hint of brown melded together in a complicated storm that mirrored her personality. Sienna was a mystery to him. Always had been, he realized. Her way of thinking was so unlike his own. Eli couldn't guess what explanation she'd have for bailing Dalton out of jail behind his back, but it'd been a mistake to walk away without giving her the opportunity.

She'd deserved better.

The chief's office opened, interrupting their conversation. Cole and Ryker emerged.

Eli rose as they approached. "Well?"

"There's no sign of the man who attacked you today," Ryker said. "Officers located the speedboat about half a mile from the marina. It'd been stolen. Crime scene techs are processing it now for fingerprints, but initial reports indicate it's been wiped down."

Eli wasn't surprised. Whoever was behind these attacks had planned and executed them with careful consideration. "He's tried to kill Sienna twice. I don't think he's done."

"The chief agreed to allow us to investigate the attacks." Cole met his gaze. "But he wants you and Sienna to back off. And Eli, he's serious about this. He's already placed a phone call to Lieutenant Rodriguez, warning her that if she doesn't reprimand you, then he's going to file an official complaint."

Eli was tired of the chief threatening his job. "What about Ruby's disappearance? Or Albert's murder?"

"That's not officially in our purview." Cole held up a hand, warding off an argument from Eli. "But if we find direct evidence that these attacks on Sienna are connected to Albert's murder or Ruby's disappearance, we're permitted to follow those leads."

Eli's gaze shot to Ryker. His friend's expression was hard. Ryker wasn't pleased with the outcome anymore than Eli was. The chief was tying their hands. Attempting to appear cooperative while preventing them from actually conducting a thorough investigation.

Nothing had changed. Eli and Sienna were still on their own as a killer hunted their every move.

ELEVEN

Thunderclouds hovered in the distance as Sienna reached in the pocket of her jacket to pull out a sugar cube for Oliver. The horse happily gobbled up the treat before nudging her for more. She ran a hand over his blaze, wishing she had time for a ride—nothing cleared her head more than racing across the fields—but there was too much to do.

Ruby was still missing. The young woman could be dead by now, the desperate phone call made to her grandmother last week sealing her fate. But Sienna wouldn't jump to that conclusion without evidence. She'd work off the assumption that Ruby was still alive. If Dallas didn't have her, then it was time to look for other suspects.

"You're up early."

The familiar timber of Eli's voice unleashed a burst of butterflies in her stomach. Sienna turned to find him crossing the dew-covered grass, the family Labrador at his side, looking like every woman's cowboy fantasy. A

Stetson covered his blond hair and a soft leather jacket molded over his broad shoulders. Every step closer increased her heart rate. The reaction was involuntary, made worse by the passionate kiss they'd shared yesterday. And she mentally berated herself for it.

Eli was right. Things were complicated enough without dragging their broken romance out of the grave.

"I couldn't sleep." Sienna tore her gaze away from the handsome lawman and fed Oliver another sugar cube. Then she wiped her hands on her jeans. "I was just taking a few minutes to enjoy the morning before I reviewed everything I had on Ruby's disappearance."

"You're allowed more than a few minutes." Eli patted Oliver's neck before hooking his arms on the wooden fence post. He took a deep breath and let it out slowly, fog puffing in front of his face. "I'd forgotten how peaceful this place is. Times like these, I think about quitting my job and buying a piece of land and just... being."

She studied him for a moment before letting her gaze drift across the land. She knew every blade of grass. Had plowed the fields alongside her parents and worked in the greenhouse. Mucked the horse stalls. Harvested the fruits and vegetables.

"There's a straightforwardness about it, isn't there?" Sienna breathed in and then out, letting the crisp air wash her clean of the troubles she'd woken up with. "Murders and kidnappings... they take a toll. It's nice to escape to a place where things are uncomplicated."

He nodded. "Exactly."

She elbowed him. "Good thing my parents have an

open door policy. Anytime you want a glimpse of farm life, they can put you to work."

Eli tossed his head back and laughed. The sound warmed Sienna straight through. She grinned up at him. There was an easy rhythm to her relationship with him. Before things became romantic, they'd been friends. Was it too much to think that one day they'd recapture at least that part of their demolished relationship?

Maybe it was. There'd been a lot of hurt.

Sienna glanced at her watch. She'd been outside for over thirty minutes. "All right. I'm heading back to review my notes on Ruby. Join me whenever you're ready. There's no rush."

"Actually, I was thinking we could work the case from the beginning. Your notes are excellent, but it's been three weeks since Ruby disappeared. People are over their shock and have had time to think about the days and weeks before the incident. Plus, I get a better feel for things when I talk to the person myself."

She could understand that. It was the same for her. "We can start with Ruby's grandmother. I'd like to question her again about the phone call she received from her granddaughter last week anyway."

"Good idea."

"I'll call her and set up a meeting this morning."

She turned to stroll back to the house, but Eli stopped her with a light touch on her forearm. "Hold on. There's something else I wanted to talk to you about." He sucked in a deep breath and seemed to brace himself. "I've been thinking about us, about what happened when we broke up. And I owe you an apology."

Sienna blinked, certain she'd misheard him. "Excuse me?"

He met her gaze. "I didn't give you a chance to explain your side of things. I was so angry about what you'd done, Sienna, so betrayed and hurt that I refused to listen." Eli dropped his hand from her arm before turning to grip the fence post. "It's not an excuse, but I learned as a kid that people who disappoint you will always do so. My father. My mom. Dalton. You were the one person in my life—other than Ryker—who I trusted implicitly. When you went behind my back... I just couldn't see any way back from that."

Sienna's heart ached so much it felt like someone had punched her. She knew he'd been hurt by her actions, but she hadn't truly understood how badly. Eli had grown up in a household of abuse, neglect, and constant chaos. It was so far removed from her own idyllic childhood, and he was so responsible and put together, she often forgot about the deep and invisible wounds that scarred him.

She stepped closer, wrapping an arm around his waist and leaning her head against his arm. "I never meant to hurt you, Eli. When Dalton called and begged me to bail him out of jail and take him to rehab, all I could think of was Harper." Her voice clogged with grief. "Not a day goes by that I don't think of her and wish she was here. Those last few months, when her addiction really spiraled out of control, were so painful. I said harsh things to her. Hateful things. I was angry and couldn't understand why she wouldn't get sober. And then... she died."

Hot tears pricked her eyes, and although Sienna tried, she couldn't hold them back. "I never got the chance to take back the mean things I'd said to her. I have to live with that every day. And I often wonder what would've happened if Harper had gone to rehab."

She might still be alive. Harper was murdered by her ex, but she'd chosen to attend a party where everyone was getting high. If she'd been sober, her choices would've been different.

Sienna fought to keep her emotions under control. She had to get through this. "When Dalton was arrested, I understood your anger. But if he died, and you never got the chance to take back the things you'd said... it would haunt you. And while I agree Dalton needed to face the consequences of his actions, taking him to rehab wouldn't have ended the criminal case against him. It would've only gotten him the help he needed to change his life for the better."

Eli was silent, but she knew he was processing her words. Sienna licked her lips. "I'm sorry for handling it badly. I should've tried harder to get you to understand my point of view, but I didn't think you would listen."

Eli swallowed hard. "I wouldn't have."

Her chin trembled. "I never meant to betray you. In my misguided way, I was protecting you."

He was quiet, his gaze on the fields beyond the fence, but he released the fence to wrap an arm around her shoulders and tuck her closer to his side. Sienna turned her face into his chest and inhaled his familiar scent. The sobs she'd buried after their breakup broke free, fueled by the stress of the last few days. She wept.

And he held her. Cradled her in his arms with all the tenderness that she needed in that moment.

Finally, when she was spent, Sienna took a few shuddering breaths. Eli cupped the back of her head, his fingers tangling with her curls. He gently wiped the remaining tears from her cheek with the soft pad of his thumb. She pulled back and caught a glimmer of tears in his eyes too.

"We should've had this conversation five years ago."

She punched him lightly on the shoulder. "I tried. You refused."

"I'm a stubborn, foolish man." He shook his head, releasing her. "So where does that leave us?"

It was a good question. In spite of their passionate kiss yesterday, Sienna wasn't sure she was ready to risk her heart all over again. Eli had cut her off without a backward glance. His abandonment, along with his refusal to hear her out, had left its own invisible scar.

And they were different people. It'd been five years. A lot had changed for them both. Sienna often made decisions quickly, but right now, she couldn't find the emotional bandwidth to sort out her feelings. "Things are so complicated. I think our focus should be on the case, as you said yesterday. Finding Ruby and catching Albert's killer are my top priorities."

He hesitated and then nodded. Eli's lips curved into a smile. "Friends?"

Relief unknotted the last bit of tension punctuating this conversation. Sienna grinned back. "Friends."

As they turned to stroll back to the house, there was a lightness in her steps that hadn't existed for a long time. Until she thought of Ruby.

Where was the young woman?

And would they find her before it was too late?

TWELVE

Amelia Morales, Ruby's grandmother, lived across town on a quiet street close to the local elementary school. Eli followed the GPS directions while staying vigilant. So far, there was no sign of Sienna's attacker, but he wouldn't let down his guard.

In the passenger seat beside him, Sienna seemed lost in her own thoughts. Her brow was furrowed, her curls tamed into a low ponytail that drew attention to the curve of her cheek and the delicate line of her jaw. The scent of her perfume filled the cab. It'd been an hour since their emotional conversation, and Eli's thoughts hadn't stopped churning.

How could he have wasted so much time?

Five years. Five long years of anger and hurt over a misunderstanding that could have been cleared up with one vulnerable conversation. Instead, Eli had blocked every attempt Sienna had made to repair their relationship. He'd let his own stubborn pride get in the way.

God, I've really screwed things up. Big-time.

Trust was a fragile thing. While Sienna had gone behind his back, her reasons were pure. She'd been trying to protect him. And he'd thanked her for it by breaking her heart. This wasn't the type of hurt that mended quickly or easily. Sienna had been right to draw a boundary around the attraction arcing between them. Despite how their conversation ended, Eli wasn't sure their friendship could be salvaged when this was all said and done.

Could he even be just friends with Sienna?

He peeked at her out of the corner of his eye. She leaned against the seat, eyes closed, long lashes resting on her cheeks. Sunlight caressed the bridge of her nose and highlighted the curve of her lips. Unable to sit still for a moment, her foot tapped in time with the music pouring from the truck's speakers.

Apples and sunshine. That was what she smelled like. The familiar scent encircled his heart and squeezed tight. Eli tried to imagine seeing her with another man. The very thought left his insides hollowed out. Yeah, no. Friendship had been the basis of their romance, but once love entered the equation, there was no going back.

He tore his gaze away from the beautiful woman sitting next to him and scanned the mirrors for any sign of trouble.

No one was following them.

At the moment.

He tightened his hand on the steering wheel, slowing for a red light in the center of town. Molly's Ice Cream

Shop sat on the corner. A sign on the sidewalk promised the best hot chocolate in the county.

When Dalton was in elementary school, there was nothing he loved more on a winter day than hot chocolate topped with mini-marshmallows. Eli would skimp and save, stealing change from the couch cushions for months, so that when report cards came out, he could buy his little brother a special treat for a job-well-done.

Back then, Dalton had been a straight-A student. Where had everything gone so wrong?

The light changed to green and Eli gently pressed on the gas. He cleared his throat. "Have you heard from Dalton?"

Sienna opened her eyes and blinked, as if his question had interrupted her line of thinking. Probably had. Eli had the sense she'd been using their car ride to mull over questions for Ruby's grandmother. Which is what he should be doing. But his mind wouldn't settle on the case at the moment.

"No." Sienna adjusted her seat belt as she sat up straighter. "After Dalton left rehab, I lost contact with him." She shot Eli a sympathetic look. "I take it from your question that you haven't seen or spoken to him either."

He sighed, his heart heavy with regret. "No. And... I don't know."

"You aren't sure if you should find him."

Eli nodded. "What if I do and he's still using? Or worse, what if his criminal record involves more than simply stealing a car?"

"Then you'll cross that bridge when you get there."

Sienna placed a hand on his forearm. "But there's just as much chance that Dalton has gotten his act together. A lot can change in five years. Isn't it better to approach the issue with positivity and hopefulness?"

That sounded like a recipe for disaster. Sienna's advice highlighted yet another difference between them. She always looked for the best in everything. Eli's childhood was spent dodging his father's flying fists and navigating his mother's dark depression, and as a result, he was trained to anticipate every injury or disappointment.

Those same skills made him an excellent Texas Ranger. But maybe they'd crippled him in his personal life. They certainly hadn't been helpful in dealing with Sienna's choices five years ago.

Eli sighed again as he turned into a quaint neighborhood. Cookie-cutter homes intermingled with older custom-designed houses. "I'll spend some time thinking about it. And praying on it."

Sienna nodded. "If you need to talk about anything, I'm here."

Her kind words only drove home the terrible way Eli had torn apart their relationship. She was carrying so much on her narrow shoulders: a murder charge, a sick father, a house that'd burned down, killers hunting her, and a missing woman. Yet Sienna didn't hesitate to offer her support. She was incredible.

Before Eli could say as much, his cell phone rang. Lieutenant Vikki Rodriguez's name flashed on the screen embedded in his truck's dash. His boss. Eli quickly pulled his vehicle over to the side of the road and fished his cell out of the cup holder to answer the call.

"Good morning, Ranger Goodwin." The lieutenant's words were clipped, but not harsh. They'd always had a good working relationship built on mutual respect. Her leadership was the entire reason Company A was such a close-knit group. "I've read the report you sent last night regarding the missing woman, Ruby Morales, and the murder of Albert Greer, along with the attacks perpetrated on Sienna Evans. You make a compelling argument why these incidents are connected, however, Chief Ramirez insists you steer clear of these investigations."

"I'm not the only one he's blocking, ma'am. He won't allow Cole or Ryker to investigate the potential connections either."

Vikki hummed and the sound of paperwork shuffling came over the line. "I'm aware. I've read their reports as well."

"Chief Ramirez believes that Ruby Morales has simply run off, but there's evidence she's being held against her will. That's not something I can ignore." He glanced at Sienna. "Nor can I allow an innocent woman to be charged with murder."

She was quiet for a long moment. "I respect your dedication to the truth, Eli, but you don't have the jurisdiction to work these cases. You also haven't been cleared by the doctors for active duty. If Chief Ramirez insists on creating a ruckus by filing an official complaint, then I won't be able to protect you from the repercussions. Do you understand?"

He could be sanctioned. Or lose his job. Eli loved being a Texas Ranger. He didn't know what life looked like without a career in law enforcement, but he couldn't abandon Sienna to save his own skin. Ruby either. He had a duty and a responsibility to see this through. Otherwise, his badge meant nothing.

"Yes, ma'am." Eli scanned his surroundings for any sign of danger. Sienna caught his gaze with eyebrows raised in silent question. He shook his head to show they were okay. "I appreciate the warning, Lieutenant."

"I suppose ordering you to stand down won't do a lick of good, will it?"

"No, ma'am, with all due respect, it won't."

Eli had never bucked the rules before. He couldn't imagine what his boss was thinking, but if the lieutenant was surprised by his response, there was no sign of it in her voice. "I've ordered Cole and Ryker to investigate the attacks against you and Sienna thoroughly. If there's any evidence these cases are linked to Albert's murder or Ruby's disappearance, then I can use that to persuade the chief to give us more leeway. In the meantime, be careful, Eli. I don't want to lose you over this."

"I pray it won't come to that."

"So do I." She hung up.

Eli replaced his cell phone in the cup holder. He put the truck back into Drive and continued on to Amelia's house.

Sienna's expression was filled with concern as she fiddled again with her seat belt. "I've said it before, but I feel the need to say it again. You don't have to do this, Eli. I'm capable of working this case on my own."

"With a killer chasing you?" He slanted a glance in her direction. "No, Sienna. Besides, if Ruby called her grandmother begging for help after she went missing, then there's evidence she's alive and being held against her will. No one in law enforcement is looking for her. I can't walk away."

He pulled up to a tiny bungalow. Crisp white shutters framed the windows, creating a contrast against the light blue siding. A late-model sedan sat in the driveway and neatly trimmed bushes spotted the flowerbeds. Birds flitted from feeder to feeder while a squirrel scurried up an oak tree. The front step was clear of leaves and pine needles. A broom rested against a rocking chair.

Eli got out of the truck and circled the vehicle to open Sienna's door. A prickle of nerves skated up the back of his spine. He turned, half-expecting to see danger heading his direction. His hand flew to the handgun holstered at his waist.

Nothing. No one was there. His gaze swept across the front of the house and then the surrounding area, searching for signs of trouble, but everything appeared as it should. An elderly man weeded his front yard three doors down while a mom wrangled her toddler into an SUV across the street. The shouts of children playing in the park attached to the elementary school carried on the wind.

"What is it?" Sienna asked. Her muscles were tense, her gaze also searching the area.

Eli rolled his shoulders. "Just a feeling." He released the hold on his holster, mentally admonishing himself for jumping at imaginary shadows. "Sorry. Maybe I'm more tense than I realized..." His attention snagged on the bungalow's front door.

It gaped open.

His entire body went on high alert as he ordered Sienna behind him and then quickly traveled up the walkway. As he grew closer, a knot tightened his belly. It was possible the older woman had simply gone out to the porch to sweep it and then hadn't closed her door well when she went back inside. But Eli wouldn't assume the best-case scenario. Not after a thug had nearly tried to kill Sienna twice. Not after Albert's murder.

Ruby had called her grandmother. Maybe someone was afraid of what she might tell them.

Inside the house was dark. The sound of a television playing the morning news spilled onto the porch. Sienna placed a hand on the center of his back between his shoulder blades as Eli pushed the door open with his foot. It was risky to call out, but he didn't have a justifiable reason to enter the home without permission. A partially open door wasn't enough. "Mrs. Morales? Are you here?"

A muffled scream came from the recesses of the house.

This time, when Eli reached for his weapon, he pulled it free of the holster.

THIRTEEN

A bolt of anger shot through Sienna and it took every ounce of strength not to barge inside and tackle the thug harming Amelia. The elderly woman was seventy-nine. A grandmother. What kind of monster would attack her in her own home?

Someone determined to silence her.

Eli must've come to the same conclusion based on the hard line of his shoulders and the tension in his muscles. This wasn't a version of him Sienna saw often, since they'd rarely worked cases together, but she recognized his focus. His determination. Law enforcement had channeled his already protective nature into a honed response. Whoever was hurting Amelia was about to have a reckoning.

"Stay behind me." Eli's voice was barely above a whisper, but his tone was commanding and sharp.

Sienna nodded. Her fingers itched for her own weapon, but the conditions of her bond forbid her from carrying any kind of gun. Instead, she hooked her index finger through the loop on the back of Eli's jeans. She wasn't used to following orders. Being a PI meant working on her own, doing things her own way. But this situation was outside the norm. Eli's sole focus needed to be on helping Amelia. The best thing Sienna could do was stay out of his way and let him do his job.

They entered the foyer. Weak sunlight streamed through gauzy curtains covering the living room windows. A floral couch, popular in the 80s, sat opposite a fireplace. The television was turned to the local news station and a cup of half-drunk coffee rested on the end table.

Sienna's pulse skyrocketed as another muffled scream filtered through the house from somewhere down the hall. Eli swept left and then right, per his training, before heading toward the sound. She kept pace with his footsteps, silently urging him to hurry. The hallway was narrow and dark. The sounds of scuffling came from the bedroom at the end. Eli's steps quickened.

They passed Ruby's bedroom. The door was open, and it looked like a tornado had blown through the space. Her mattress was overturned and tossed to the side. Clothes spilled from the drawers and books had been toppled from shelves. Even the pillows had been torn open, stuffing lying in heaps like discarded cotton balls. Sienna barely had a moment to register the destruction before continuing down the hall after Eli.

He halted outside the primary bedroom door, holding up a hand to show Sienna should stay put. She released her hold on his belt loop. The sounds of scuffling, as if a fight was taking place, filtered out of the room. Her heart pounded.

Please protect Amelia and Eli, Lord. Guide our decisions with Your wisdom so we can do Your bidding.

Sienna's breath caught as Eli entered the bedroom, gun at the ready. "Police! Freeze!"

From her position in the hallway, Sienna saw a man wearing jeans and a black long-sleeved T-shirt barrel across the bedroom. He collided with Eli like a linebacker and the two men slammed into the opposite wall before toppling to the ground taking the nightstand with them.

Eli's gun flew from his hand. The weapon landed on the carpet, just inside the doorway.

Sienna didn't hesitate. She scooped up the Glock as the sound of flesh hitting flesh filled the bedroom. The men rolled across the carpet, throwing punches, each one attempting to gain the upper hand. Eli was strong and quick, but he was still recovering from being shot months ago. Plus the attacker outweighed him by nearly fifty pounds.

Sienna pointed the weapon, but the men were a blur of activity. "Freeze!"

No one heeded her command.

The dresser shuddered as the men collided with it. A framed photograph of Ruby toppled from the surface. It pelted the attacker on the head on its way to the ground. If he felt it, there was no sign. He kneed Eli in the groin and then whipped out a knife, holding it to the Texas Ranger's throat.

"Stop!" This time Sienna's command carried across the room. She shifted so the masked man was facing down the barrel of the gun. "Drop the knife."

The masked man bared his teeth. Fear threatened to overtake her. One slice and he'd cut right through Eli's carotid artery. Her ex would bleed out in seconds. Nothing could stop it.

Sienna swallowed. Now was not the time to think about how many ways this could go wrong. Instead, she met the attacker's hardened gaze with one of her own. "I will shoot you if I have to."

It wasn't an empty threat. Sienna didn't relish the thought of taking anyone's life, but if it meant saving Eli, then she would do what was necessary without hesitation. She made sure steel coated her next words. "Drop the knife. Now!"

For a moment, Sienna feared he would ignore her, but then the attacker eased the blade away from Eli's throat. He tossed it on the carpet.

Eli didn't waste a second. He flipped the man onto the ground, pulling his wrists behind his back, and securing them with handcuffs.

Sienna let go of the breath she was holding and lowered the gun. "You okay?"

"Fine."

The word came out harsh. Sienna sensed he wasn't angry with her, but was with himself. Eli had lost the upper hand in the fight. That wasn't something a man like him could let go of easily. Thankfully, his pride seemed to have taken the worst of it. He sported a cut on his cheek and a darkening bruise along his chin, but otherwise appeared unharmed.

Eli patted down the intruder for any other weapons, but came up empty-handed. The man didn't have any ID either.

Once he was finished, Sienna extended the gun for him to take. Her gaze swept the bedroom, but there was no sign of Ruby's grandmother. "Amelia?"

Eli tilted his head toward the bathroom. "In there. She and the intruder were wrestling over the door when we arrived."

Sienna crossed the carpet as Eli called for backup while keeping his weapon trained on the masked intruder. The door to the bathroom was closed tight. Sienna knocked on the wood. "Amelia? It's Sienna Evans. You're safe now. Can you open the door?"

Shuffling came from inside the bathroom, and then the lock snicked open. Amelia appeared. She wore a housedress and one slipper. Her normally tidy gray hair was flying in all directions. Thick silver tape hung from the corner of her mouth and rope dangled from one wrist. A huge bruise marred her cheek. More covered her bare arms.

Relief flickered across her face. She swayed.

Sienna caught the frail woman before she hit the tile floor. "Eli, ask for an ambulance." She barely registered his voice as he complied with her order. Her sole focus was on assisting Amelia to the bed so she could sit down.

"I'm fine." Amelia's whole body trembled and her complexion was pale.

"You've been through an ordeal. It's okay not to be fine." Sienna snagged the comforter off the bed and wrapped it around Amelia's shoulders. Shock was a real threat. It could kill the older woman.

Tears filled Amelia's brown eyes. She grabbed Sienna's hand. "Thank God you came when you did." She licked her lips. "He rang the doorbell. I answered without looking through the peephole, thinking it was my neighbor who often comes over for breakfast." The tears spilled over her wrinkled cheeks. "I realized my mistake too late. He pushed his way into the house. Punched me and then tied me up. I got free while he was searching Ruby's bedroom, and ran for the bathroom to lock myself inside, but he must've heard me."

That explained why they were wrestling over the bathroom door when Eli arrived. Amelia's cries had been muffled by the tape covering her mouth. Sienna gently removed the offending item from the corner of the older woman's mouth where it dangled after she tried to rip it off once she was locked in the bathroom. "You're safe now. Everything is going to be okay."

The words of comfort seemed to provide Amelia strength. She straightened her spine, turning her gaze toward the intruder. "Who is he?"

"An excellent question." Eli ripped off the attacker's mask. The man had a square face with pebbled cheeks and chapped lips. His bald head reflected the sunlight streaming through the bedroom windows. A cut from the photograph frame dripped blood down his scalp and around his ear. Bruises from the fight spotted his cheeks and chin. His pupils were dilated.

Was he high? Sienna suspected as much. Her sister's eyes had looked the same when she was using. It also explained why the man didn't seem bothered by his injuries. He probably hadn't felt a thing during the fight. Judging from the veins popping in the man's forearms and the acne on his face, his recreational drug use included steroids.

"Who are you?" Eli barked out.

The man scowled and kept his mouth shut tight. Sienna didn't recognize him. From the look on Eli's face, neither did he. Was this the same man who'd attempted to kill them in the marina? Was he also Albert's murderer? Ruby's kidnapper?

Amelia studied the attacker's face for a long moment, her brow crinkled, as if she was trying to drudge up a memory from the recesses of her mind. Then she gasped. "You're from Fresh Start. I remember seeing you at a fundraiser a few months ago. Ruby told me your name was Jesse."

"Fresh Start?" Shock rippled through Sienna. The non-profit organization provided support and encouragement to those who suffered from addiction. They helped former addicts find jobs and housing, provided meals, ran vocational classes. There was counseling too. A few members lived on premises in the upstairs bedrooms in exchange for assisting at the center.

Ruby worked there as an administrative assistant. Sienna hadn't had a chance to interviewed any of her colleagues, or her boss, the director of Fresh Start, Gideon Wade yet.

Amelia rose. Her expression shifted from fear to fiery determination. "Where's Ruby? What have you done with my granddaughter?"

"I ain't done nothin' to Ruby," he snarled. "I want a lawyer."

Sienna scoffed. The man might be high as a kite, but his brain cells were still firing. Sirens from approaching first responders wailed in the distance. They would be here soon, and once that happened, she wouldn't have a chance to question the intruder again. She stepped into his line of sight. "The only thing I'm concerned about is finding Ruby. If you know where she is, you need to tell us so we can help her."

"I don't know anything. I was hired to..." His mouth clamped shut as his gaze darted around the room. "I can't say any more. I'm a dead man if I do."

Hired? A streak of horror ripped through Sienna. She shared a quick glance with Eli and saw her own fears reflected in his gaze. Then he focused back on the hand-cuffed criminal.

"I'm a Texas Ranger. Whoever you're scared of, I can help." He crouched down to look the man in the eye. "I can make sure you're protected."

The wail of sirens grew louder. Jesse swallowed hard and shook his head. "No way."

"What were you looking for in Ruby's room?" Sienna tried a last ditch effort to get the man to talk. Time was running out for Ruby. She could feel it in her bones.

Whatever the young woman had stumbled into, it was bad. They needed something more to help narrow the search for her. "Whatever it was, you didn't find it. That's why you needed her grandmother alive. To tell you where Ruby hid it."

Jesse pressed his lips together. No amount of questions or pleading would convince him to talk. They were wasting time.

Sienna turned away from him in disgust and went back to Amelia. "Do you know what he was looking for?"

"The only thing I can think of is Ruby's computer. I put it in my closet for safekeeping after she went missing. Top shelf."

Sienna had been through Ruby's computer once. Nothing in her social media accounts or search history appeared out of the ordinary, but there was a strong possibility she'd missed something during her initial scan. She hurried through the bathroom and went into the closet.

"Sienna." Eli's warning tone didn't slow her steps. He followed her as far as the bathroom, keeping his weapon trained on Jesse. The criminal was sitting on the floor next to the dresser, his head between his legs. "We can't remove evidence."

She found the laptop right where Amelia said it would be. Sienna scooped it up and tucked the device into her jacket, zipping it closed. "No lectures, Eli. You're already operating outside of the law. Taking Ruby's computer before the police get here makes sense. Now help me slip out to the truck before someone notices."

FOURTEEN

"Ruby suspected something illegal was happening at Fresh Start."

Eli's attention shot away from the background check he was currently conducting on Jesse O'Neal, the attacker from Amelia Morales's home. It was illegal for him to use his ranger resources, but Sienna had access to a paid database that provided much of the same information. Jesse had a long rap sheet that included numerous drug charges, assaults, and thefts. He'd been court-ordered into rehab three months ago following a possession charge. His current address was Fresh Start.

Sienna tapped on the keyboard of Ruby's laptop. They'd managed to smuggle it out of the house without any of the officers noticing. A pinprick of guilt stabbed Eli. He hated operating outside the boundaries of the law. Taking the laptop was a clear violation of protocol, but turning it over to the Sandalwood Police Department would've left them in the dark. Since Chief Ramirez made it clear he wouldn't reopen Ruby's missing person's case, Eli was placed in an untenable position.

Having integrity meant doing the right thing, no matter the consequences. Based on everything Eli knew so far, Ruby was still alive but in grave trouble. If saving her meant breaking a few rules along the way... then so be it.

"How do you know she suspected something illegal was going on?" Eli rose from his chair and circled around to Sienna's side of the dining room table. It was littered with crumpled notes, loose-leaf papers, and discarded coffee mugs.

Her mane of curls was piled into a messy bun. An off-the-shoulder sweater revealed the delicate line of her collarbone and inches of soft skin. Without warning, Eli's brain imagined walking up behind her and placing a kiss on the curve of her neck while his fingers trailed along the edges of that bare shoulder.

"Did you hear me?" Sienna glanced up from the laptop screen.

Belatedly, Eli realized she'd been talking, and he hadn't heard a word. He dragged his attention away from her and focused on the laptop screen. "Sorry. I was lost in thought for a moment. What did you say?"

"Ruby handled a lot of things at Fresh Start. She organized fundraisers, did some of the bookkeeping, scheduled the classes and teachers. Last year, Ruby noticed there was a lot of money coming in through anonymous donations. Then she started keeping track of the invoices for items the charity supposedly purchased for fundraising events. The numbers are inflated. It looks like someone was laundering money through Fresh Start."

Eli pulled up a chair next to Sienna, his heart racing. Laundering money through charities wasn't a new concept. Criminals had been doing it for years.

He scanned the documents on Sienna's laptop. There were photographs of donations and invoices, along with a diary of sorts, cataloging the suspicious things Ruby had uncovered. "All of this was on her computer?"

"Yes. I screwed up. When I checked Ruby's computer, I looked at her social media and search history. Nothing appeared out of the ordinary, so I moved on to interviewing her friends. That was an oversight. I should've checked her documents as well." Sienna gestured to the laptop screen. "This was tucked inside another file with a bunch of schoolwork."

"She purposely hid it."

Sienna nodded. "This may have been what Ruby tried to tell her grandmother when she called last week." Her mouth flattened. "I should've been more thorough."

"Hindsight is always 20/20. Besides, you already had a suspect when Ruby's friends told you about Dallas stalking her. I would've focused on him too." He leaned back. "Who runs Fresh Start?"

Sienna clicked over to a website. A man with dark hair and a brilliant smile appeared on screen. "Meet Gideon Wade. Thirty years old. No criminal record. His father is on the city council, his mother is a judge. Gideon's family is friendly with the mayor and the governor." She flipped through a set of pictures, stopping at one of Gideon with Chief Ramirez. "He's also friends with the police chief."

Eli studied the photograph. It'd been taken at some kind of fundraising event. "I'm sure the police chief attends many functions. He is an important member of the community. It doesn't necessarily mean anything."

Sienna sighed. "I know, but Chief Ramirez's reluctance to pursue Ruby's case is troubling. At this point, it also doesn't make sense. Logically, he should be pursuing every lead, especially after the newspaper article that came out this morning and the attack against us at the marina. But he insists on keeping the Texas Rangers on a leash. It feels like he's covering something up."

He couldn't argue with her logic, but jumping to conclusions without evidence was a terrible idea. "Right now, we don't know if Gideon is involved in Ruby's disappearance. Let's follow the facts and see where they take us. We need to interview Gideon."

"Agreed. We also need to check these invoices Ruby took photos of. I want to know if these companies are real, and if so, who owns them. Unfortunately, it'll take time. Some of them are registered in states that hide the shareholders' identity from the public. It'll take subpoena power to discover who they are."

"Good thing you know someone with subpoena power." Ryker entered the dining room, carrying a mug of coffee and a plate of sandwiches. He set the food down on the table. "Sienna's mom promised homemade brownies if we eat these first. I, for one, am taking her up on that offer."

Eli's stomach growled. He reached for a sub stuffed with turkey, lettuce, and tomato. Sienna's mom could turn simple sandwiches into a gourmet treat. And her brownies were out of this world. "Where's Cole?"

"I left him back at the police station, like you asked. He'd have a heart attack if he knew you'd stolen Ruby's laptop."

"We didn't *steal* the laptop." Sienna reached for her own sandwich and a napkin. "Borrowed is a more appropriate word. In fact, you're welcome to take the computer with you when you go." She grinned at Ryker. "I've copied everything onto another hard drive."

He snorted. "I doubt the police chief—or Cole—will appreciate the distinction."

Before this case, Eli wouldn't have either, which is why he didn't call Cole, who was a stickler for the rules. Instead, he phoned Ryker. His best friend had always pushed against every boundary or rule he'd come across. In his youth, he'd been reckless. Now he was more careful about his choices, but his core character hadn't changed. Ryker would always be something of a rebel.

Much like Sienna. She made up her own set of guidelines and followed them without apology, unwilling to go with the status quo if it ultimately resulted in the wrong outcome.

Once again, Eli was struck by the notion that his strict adherence to the rules might be hindering rather than helping him. It made him too quick to judge. Too rigid and hard. Of course, he would never willfully be a rule breaker, but there were times and circumstances that couldn't fit neatly into a black-and-white guideline.

Like now.

He took a bite of his sandwich, the crusty bread giving way with a satisfying crunch as an explosion of flavor erupted on his tongue. Mayonnaise smeared onto his cheek. He wiped it away with a napkin before filling Ryker in on everything they'd learned. "What's going on at the police station?"

Ryker frowned. "Jesse's still refusing to talk. He did confess to being hired by someone to break into the house, but is refusing to say who. Chief Ramirez believes the Greer boys are responsible. Or someone in their family is."

"Why would Albert's cousins go after Amelia?" Sienna frowned. "That makes no sense if they believe I'm the one responsible for his death."

"The chief doesn't have an answer for that yet. I think he's getting closer to accepting that Albert's murder and Ruby's disappearance are connected, but we need more evidence to convince him."

Eli wiped the last of the crumbs from his hands. "Hopefully, these notes we've uncovered on Ruby's computer will do the trick." He tossed the crumpled napkin on his empty plate. "We're going to interview Gideon Wade, the director of Fresh Start, tomorrow morning. Can you start digging into these invoices Ruby copied? Let's see if these companies are real, and if so, who owns them."

"I can try. Chief Ramirez may fight me on it though." Ryker's expression grew speculative. "Any chance there's a link between Albert and Fresh Start?"

Sienna frowned. "That's an excellent question." She started tapping away on her laptop, and moments later, gave out a squeal of excitement. "Albert taught classes on commercial fishing for Fresh Start. He's been doing it for the last two years." She turned back to face the men. "I assumed that Albert saw something on the night of Ruby's disappearance, but maybe that's not true. Maybe he observed something while at Fresh Start."

"Something that became significant after Ruby's disappearance," Eli said, following her chain of thought.

It was a breakthrough. A big one. His heart rate picked up speed. "Let's talk this through. Ruby suspects someone is laundering money through Fresh Start. She starts investigating and keeps records. Somehow, Albert overhears a conversation or figures out something is going on. Then Ruby disappears."

"The police chief refuses to investigate properly," Sienna adds. "When Ruby's grandmother receives a desperate phone call from her granddaughter, she hires me. I start digging into the case, and that makes Ruby's kidnapper nervous. On top of that, I suspect Albert attempted to blackmail the person who kidnapped Ruby."

It made sense with everything they knew about the fisherman. Albert had gotten in trouble for blackmailing people before. "It would explain how Ruby's kidnapper knew about the meeting between you and Albert."

Sienna nodded. "Albert told him. As a threat to convince him to pay up."

"Except it backfires. Ruby's kidnapper decides to get rid of two problems at the same time. He steals your gun and frames you for Albert's murder. That way his blackmailer is dead and you're sitting in jail on a murder charge."

"The plan would have worked." Sienna shot him a look of appreciation that warmed Eli straight through. "Except you showed up and bailed me out of jail. Now he has a PI and a Texas Ranger chasing him down. He moves into clean-up mode and hires Jesse." She turned to Ryker. "Do we know if Jesse is responsible for the other attacks against me?"

"No. We're still reviewing the evidence, but there's nothing definitive connecting him to the prior attacks." His expression was grim. "I think we need to assume whoever hired him might have others on the payroll."

Eli didn't like the thought of that. It was bad enough that one man was trying to kill Sienna. The thought of multiple people coming for her... his chest squeezed tight.

"There's another problem." Ryker tilted his head. "Why does Ruby's kidnapper go to all this trouble? Wouldn't it make more sense to kill her and be done with it?"

Eli paused, considering his colleague's point. "Not if the kidnapper needs her alive for some reason."

"What reason?"

"I don't know, but I intend to find out."

FIFTEEN

Fresh Start was located near the marina. It'd once been a commercial warehouse. Effort and money had turned the building into a modern red-bricked structure with three stories and oversized windows. Leafy plants in terra-cotta pots provided shade for a picnic bench in the small grassy yard between the sidewalk and the entrance.

It was an oasis in an otherwise desolate area of town. Most of the other warehouses were vacant, abandoned after the fishing industry died out. Dark streaks created by time and water damage marred many of the gray buildings.

Sienna shuddered as an icy wind whipped down the collar of her jacket. She disliked this section of town. Albert's murder had only solidified the feeling. Would she ever smell salty air again and not remember the poor man's body falling out of the chair?

Her gaze drifted toward the fishing vessels docked a

short distance away. Albert's boat was barely visible from where she stood. The crime scene tape had been removed and a makeshift dock had replaced the one the speed boat tore apart a few days ago.

"This place hasn't changed much." Eli said, joining her on the cracked sidewalk. He settled his cowboy hat on his head to block out the morning sunshine. "I thought the mayor started an initiative to change these old warehouses into something the community could use."

"It didn't go far." She raised the collar of her coat. "It's a shame since these buildings are so close to the marina. Revitalizing the warehouses would help with tourism. Rumor has it a corporation swept in and bought a bunch of them a few years ago but never did anything afterward."

Eli's nose wrinkled. "Investors looking to get rich when the property values increase."

"Probably."

Sienna strolled up the sidewalk to the entrance. The lobby was decorated in soft blues and soothing grays. As luck would have it, Gideon was behind the front counter, speaking to the receptionist.

He glanced up as they approached. Recognition flared briefly in his expression before he hid it away. Since his gaze was locked on both Sienna and Eli, it was hard to determine which one of them had caused the reaction.

Either was possible. Eli had worked as a Texas Ranger for years in Sandalwood before moving away. As for Sienna, she'd created a name for herself in the county and surrounding towns by successfully investigating difficult cases. Most residents knew who she was, even if it was by reputation only. Of course, with Albert's murder, she'd become infamous for all the wrong reasons.

She plastered on a polite smile. "Mr. Wade?"

"Yes." He straightened to his full height. Soft brown eyes, youthful features, and round cheeks gave him the appearance of a younger man. He wore a button-up dress shirt, sleeves rolled to the elbows, and slacks. His straight brown hair was left to grow long on top and a swatch of it fell over his forehead. He brushed it away. "Can I help you?"

"My name is Sienna Evans, and this is my colleague Elijah Goodwin. We've been hired by Ruby's grandmother to investigate her disappearance and were hoping to ask you a few questions."

Not a flicker of surprise or confusion creased Gideon's features. Sienna had the gut feeling he'd been expecting them. Had he heard about the investigation through the Sandalwood grapevine? Or had he hired Jesse, and once the man was arrested, figured it would be a matter of time before Sienna and Eli landed on his doorstep?

"Let's chat in my office." Gideon patted the receptionist on the shoulder. "Iris, hold my calls, please."

He used a key card to access a door leading from the lobby into a long hallway. Classrooms outfitted with desks and whiteboards jutted off either side. A glass-walled library sat next to a computer room. The nonprofit hummed with activity as people moved from one place to another, but no one seemed in a rush. More than one person greeted Gideon with a brilliant smile. He never failed to respond with a kind word or a question about how classes were going.

Sienna watched each interaction with interest. She lengthened her steps to match Gideon's as they passed a large staircase. Photographs and magazine articles about the organization graced the opposite wall. A trophy case with various awards flanked the entrance to a large conference room. "I've heard about Fresh Start, but I didn't know the organization was this big. How many students do you have here?"

"Currently enrollment is 200. We offer vocational training in everything from plumbing to car mechanics, but most of the members avail themselves of our other services. We run support meetings, provide counseling, interview training, resume assistance, and a lending library."

"Are all of your members recovering addicts?" Eli asked.

"Yes." Pride filled his voice. "We've helped over one thousand people since opening our doors ten years ago. I can't take all the credit, of course. Our founding director, Matthew Lyons, retired two years ago. That's when I took over."

Gideon stopped in front of a door and used his key card to open the lock. The office was modestly sized but decorated with a modern touch. Oversized windows provided stunning views of the rocky shore and the ocean. Elegant wingback chairs faced a sleek black desk topped with a state-of-the-art computer.

Eli placed a hand on the small of Sienna's back as they crossed over the threshold. The simple touch was gentlemanly and utterly distracting. She quickly moved away to claim one of the visitor's chairs. "Lovely office."

"Thank you. My fiancée decorated it." Gideon smiled and pointed to a framed photograph of him with a gorgeous, long-legged blonde woman. Sienna instantly recognized the couple in the photograph with them. Governor Whitman and his wife.

The family resemblance to Gideon's fiancée was obvious. She had to be the governor's daughter. Still, Sienna played ignorant. "Is this the governor and his wife?"

"It is. The Whitmans have been proud supporters of Fresh Start for years. That's how Penelope and I met. She's their daughter." Gideon sat in the curved chair behind his desk. "She's also the governor's campaign manager. Rumor has it, he's planning on running for senate next." He winked. "Although you didn't hear that from me."

Sienna placed a hand over her lips and mimed zipping them. "I won't tell a soul."

Gideon's tone was playful, but he wanted to make it clear he had friends in high places. A threat? A warning? It was hard to tell. Something about him didn't add up. He appeared youthful and eagerly honest, but she sensed there was a cunning mind behind that baby face.

"Now then, you wanted to ask me some questions

about Ruby." Gideon's gaze drifted between Sienna and Eli. "I've been meaning to reach out to her grandmother for weeks, but things have been so busy around here. We're constantly short-staffed. Like most nonprofits, we have a tiny operating budget and our staff is small. Ruby was one of the best administrative assistants I've ever had. She had a talent for organizing, and I miss having her around."

It was odd Gideon hadn't called to offer his support after she disappeared. Once again, Sienna had the impression he was attempting to manipulate them. She held his gaze. "What kind of work did she do for you?"

"A bit of everything. Fundraising, organizing events, scheduling teachers. Whatever help we needed, she was always happy to pitch in."

Eli removed his cowboy hat and rested it on one knee. "Did you find it strange when Ruby just up and disappeared?"

Gideon waved a slim hand one way and then the other in a seesaw motion. "She was unusually responsible, but also young, with a lot of things on her plate. A demanding master's program, caring for an elderly grandmother, and a full-time job. So much expectation can become overwhelming.

"I was especially concerned about Ruby in the last few weeks before she disappeared. It didn't seem she was getting enough sleep and was losing weight. I'd planned to have a conversation with her about cutting back on her hours here, but never got the chance." He shrugged. "I spoke with Chief Ramirez a few weeks ago. He confirmed Ruby's debit card has been used recently. We both figured she needed a break from life and would pop back up in a few weeks."

"Losing weight and not sleeping?" Sienna leaned forward. "Sounds like she was worried about something. Do you know what it was?"

He frowned. "She never mentioned anything specific. I know her classes were unusually hard last semester, and she struggled to keep up with the workload."

She kept her gaze locked on his face. "What about here? Did Ruby have any troubles with anyone or anything at Fresh Start?"

"If she did, she didn't mention it to me," he answered smoothly.

The words came too easily, as if they were well-rehearsed. Sienna didn't believe him for a moment. If Ruby uncovered someone was laundering money through the charity, she probably would've taken it straight to Gideon. He was the director. Unless... unless she'd suspected he was involved.

Sienna's heart broke for Ruby. It must've been awful to discover someone—or multiple people—were using the charity to hide criminal activity. The only thing worse was not knowing who to trust with the information. No wonder she'd been losing sleep.

"You mentioned Ruby scheduled the teachers." Eli had taken out his new cell phone and was typing notes. "What was her interaction with Albert Greer like?"

His forehead crinkled. "I'm not sure she ever interacted with Albert. He taught here a couple of years ago, but it's been a while." He swiped an invisible fleck off the slick desktop. "Not to speak ill of the dead, but Albert wasn't one of our favorite teachers. He yelled at the students, and after many complaints, we let him go."

Sienna wasn't surprised. Albert's rough attitude was well known. "His name is still listed as a teacher on your website."

He waved a hand dismissively. "Our website needs a complete overhaul. We add photos from events and update our fundraising campaigns, but the rest of the pages are sadly out-of-date. It's one of the many things on my to-do list." He frowned. "Why are you asking about Albert? Do you believe his death is connected to Ruby's disappearance?"

"It's an avenue we're pursuing."

He arched a brow. "The police chief seems certain you're responsible for his death, Ms. Evans. You've been charged with his murder." The polite veneer melted away from Gideon's face. His lips hardened. "I'm concerned you're attempting to link Albert's murder to Ruby's disappearance for your own sake. No one benefits from that, especially Mrs. Morales, who must be worried sick about her granddaughter."

A flare of anger heated Sienna's blood, but she kept the evidence of it from bleeding into her voice. "My repu-tation as a private investigator speaks for itself. I would never use a family's pain for my own benefit." She met his gaze. "We have evidence that Ruby is in trouble. Our intention is to find her and put whoever harmed her behind bars."

The room crackled with a silent tension.

Then Gideon slicked on a smile. "Well, I certainly hope you're wrong about Ruby, and she's simply taking a break from an overwhelming schedule." He pushed away from the desk and rose. "Forgive me if I sound accusatory, Ms. Evans. It's not my intention. Ruby is a special young woman. I know her grandmother loves her dearly, and I've seen people taken advantage of when they are vulnerable."

His apology rang with sincerity, and Sienna questioned her own intuition. Perhaps she'd misread him. "My own sister's murder was unsolved for years. I wouldn't wish that kind of pain on anyone. All I'm interested in is finding Ruby. To that end, we'd like to question some of your staff."

"No." His tone brooked no argument. "Neither of you are law enforcement officers and I won't subject my staff to questioning that would disrupt the important work we're doing."

Eli rose to his full height. "Don't you want to do everything you can to help find Ruby?"

"I have. I've answered your questions and made my staff available to Chief Ramirez." He circled the desk and headed for the door. "I promise to alert the authorities if I learn anything that can help. In the meantime, allow me to escort you back to the front desk. Our offices are a maze for newcomers."

Sienna wasn't quite ready to leave yet. "What about Jesse O'Neal? Do you know him?"

Gideon's posture stiffened even more. He turned to face them, anger etched across his features. "Mr. O'Neal was a member of our community, but hasn't been for quite some time. I was informed of his arrest by Chief Ramirez, who warned me you'd stop by to ask questions about him. While I can appreciate the concern over Ruby's whereabouts, I won't have my charity's good name besmirched. Attempting to link Albert's murder or Jesse's attack on Mrs. Morales to Fresh Start won't be tolerated. We have nothing to do with those terrible incidents."

He marched to the door and opened it wide. Sienna hesitated but decided she'd pushed things far enough. Gideon was protective of his charity's good name, which was understandable, but was his reaction genuine? Or was he simply nervous they would uncover his money-laundering scheme?

She needed more information about him, and it wouldn't happen now. The meeting was over. Sienna shared a glance with Eli before heading for the door. She crossed over the threshold and rounded the corner, her steps fueled by frustration and disappointment. They were no closer to uncovering Ruby's whereabouts. She'd hoped to question staff members, but that wasn't to be.

Sienna ran smack into a wall of muscle. With a yelp, she fell back. Two warm hands grasped her elbows lightly, halting her momentum before she landed on her backside. She tossed curls out of her eyes, the face of the man still holding onto her arms coming into full view.

She gasped. The slope of his mouth and the curve of his jaw were all too familiar, as were the sky-blue shade of his eyes. Sienna's brain froze, unable to process what her eyes were telling her. It couldn't be. But it was.

The man she'd run into was Dalton.

Eli's younger brother.

SIXTEEN

Shock ripped through Eli. It took every ounce of his training to keep the emotion from leaching onto his face as he stared at his younger brother.

Dalton looked so much like their father. Nearly a carbon copy down to the chestnut highlights in his hair and the slope of his nose. Time had etched faint lines along the corners of his eyes and deepened the cleft in his chin. He'd put on weight—at least sixty pounds—most of it sheer muscle. For a moment, flashes of hurled insults mingled with the memory of flying fists as Dalton's image melded with their father's in Eli's mind.

He blinked, willing the thoughts away, all too aware that Gideon was standing in the hallway, observing this family reunion with a slanted look of suspicion.

"Hello, Dalton."

His brother gaped like a fish out of water, his gaze darting between Sienna and Eli before he gathered his senses. A brilliant smile broke out across his face. "Eli. Sienna. What are you doing here?"

Sienna seemed to have lost the ability to speak. Eli shifted forward, forcing Dalton to drop his hands from her arms. His baby brother and his ex had never been anything more than friends, but the sight of Dalton touching her sent a wave of protectiveness streaking through Eli. Or maybe it was caused by Gideon. The meeting in the director's office had bordered on hostile, and Eli didn't like the way the man looked at Sienna. Like a bug he intended to squash.

"Mr. Goodwin and Ms. Evans wanted to ask me a few questions." Gideon waved a finger between the three of them. "How do you all know each other?"

"Dalton is an old friend." Eli's tone was neutral, belying the emotions roiling his insides like a clothes dryer on high. He had the unexpected urge to close the distance and embrace his brother in a bear hug. Gideon's presence held him back. Some internal warning bell kept Eli from admitting he and Dalton were related.

He didn't know what was going on at Fresh Start. Evidence suggested someone—or multiple people—were laundering money. Albert had been shot. Ruby was missing. The last thing Eli wanted to do was put his brother at risk by revealing the true nature of their relationship.

Then again… his brother could be involved. Dalton wore a shirt with the Fresh Start logo etched on the sleeve. The silver name tag pinned on the right side of his blazer bore his full name. Dalton Hutchinson.

The brothers didn't have the same last name since

their biological dads were different. It had never affected their interaction. In fact, Eli often forgot they didn't share the same father since they were raised by the same man. Eli's biological dad had died before he was ever born. His mother had remarried when he was two to Dalton's father.

In this moment, Eli was grateful for the fact that he had a different last name than Dalton, but it was incredibly painful to see his brother's smile fade from view. It was replaced with hurt.

Dalton glanced at his boss. "Yes. Eli and Sienna are old friends." He tried to recover his smile. "Are you guys taking a tour?"

"Actually, Mr. Wade was walking us out, but he has a meeting to get to." Sienna had recovered her wits. She flashed Dalton an encouraging grin while linking her arm through his. "There wasn't time for a tour. I'd love for you to give us one, if you can."

"I'd be happy to."

Gideon looked ready to argue, but then decided against it. He offered a tight smile. "I'll leave y'all to it then. Dalton, don't forget about our staff meeting in half an hour."

"Yes, sir."

Gideon left without a backward glance. The man was strange. One moment he seemed friendly and gracious, the next annoyed and hostile. Eli had never met Ruby, but he had a difficult time imagining the young woman had gotten along well with the mercurial director.

He shoved those thoughts aside as he focused back on

his little brother. Dalton looked healthy. It was a relief. Eli hadn't realized until this moment how much he'd silently and secretly worried about Dalton for the last five years. Where he was. What he was doing. If he was sober. Face-to-face with proof of Dalton's recovery nearly brought tears to his eyes. He blinked them back, pointing to the name tag on Dalton's blazer. "You're a counselor?"

He nodded. "I've been working for Fresh Start for the last year." Dalton's gaze swept over Eli. "You look good."

"So do you." Again the urge to hug his brother overwhelmed Eli, but he held back. "I didn't know you were living in Sandalwood."

"Neither did I," Sienna chimed in.

A blush crept up Dalton's neck and his gaze drifted to the floor. "It took me a long time to get sober and I've kept a low profile since." He lifted his gaze, squinting at Sienna and Eli. "What are you guys doing here, anyway? Does this have anything to do with Ruby's disappearance?"

Dalton had always been brilliant. Eli wasn't surprised his brother had put two and two together.

"Yes." Sienna pitched her voice low. "I've been hired by Ruby's grandmother to investigate her disappearance. We interviewed Gideon, but he wasn't very helpful. I wasn't joking about the tour. I'd love to see everything and you can fill us in on what you know about Ruby."

"Let's wait until after the tour to discuss it." He glanced over his shoulder as if making sure Gideon wasn't standing behind them. "We can talk more freely in the parking lot."

Dalton spent the next twenty minutes showing them the facilities. Like Gideon's office, the rest of the building was decorated with a modern touch and state-of-the-art electronics. Eli took it all in with a careful eye. "There must be thousands of dollars in computer equipment in this place."

"We're the only facility of its kind in five counties, and we've been blessed with generous donors." Dalton escorted them toward the lobby. "Unfortunately, addiction is something that affects a lot of families. The more support we can provide, the better for the community. Our mission is to give former addicts the skills they need to change their lives for the better. Jobs are only a small part of it. This is also a place where they can find a community of supportive people who know exactly what it's like to struggle with addiction." He stopped in front of a door and used a key card to open it. "This is my office."

The space was small but comfortable. Dalton had shed the modern decor for more traditional furniture. A well-loved leather couch, an old-fashioned desk, and bookshelves weighted down with novels took up most of the space. His window overlooked the parking lot.

Eli recognized the baseball bat sitting in the center of the bookshelf. After Dalton got out of rehab the first time, they went to a game and met with some of the players who were gracious enough to sign the bat. The memory was a happy one and sent a piercing longing through Eli's chest.

He touched the bat. "You kept it."

"Of course." Dalton sounded surprised, but his

expression mirrored Eli's own sadness. "I keep meaning to go to another game but haven't found the time."

"Me neither." Baseball was one of the things that bonded them. Eli had played in high school, as had Dalton. For a while. Before drugs and bad choices took him down a different path. Since their estrangement, Eli hadn't had the heart to even watch a game.

He cleared his throat and tamped down on the emotions threatening to swell as they exited Dalton's office and continued to the lobby. "Did Fresh Start help you?"

"No. I had to go through rehab twice more since the last time we saw each other. The final straw was when I overdosed and nearly died. I fought to get clean and stay that way. I've been sober for three years. Went back to school, got my bachelor's degree in psychology."

"You graduated from college in less than three years?" Sienna asked, incredulous.

Dalton grinned. "I was determined. Eli can tell you: once I put my mind to something, I do it."

He snorted and grinned back. "Ain't that the truth."

They exited the building. The sun had risen in the sky but did little to erase the frigid temperatures. Thunderclouds hovered on the horizon. Meteorologists predicted rain this afternoon. Most of the evening too. Looked like they would be right.

Eli settled his cowboy hat on his head. He was eager to hear what his brother had to say about Ruby.

Apparently, so was Sienna. She tucked her hands in

her pockets and kept her voice pitched low as she said, "Okay, Dalton, spill it. What do you know about Ruby?"

"First of all, I never believed she simply left town, no matter what the police chief claimed. Ruby was far too responsible for that, and she adored her grandmother. I've never heard anyone speak so lovingly about someone. I told as much to Chief Ramirez, but he didn't take my observations seriously."

"You're not the only one." Sienna rolled her eyes.

"There's more. Ruby was struggling with something in the days before her disappearance." Dalton's expression was grave. "I caught her crying and tried to get her to confide in me what was going on, but she refused."

"Do you think it had something to do with Gideon?" Eli asked.

His brother glanced back at the building. "I don't know. I've worked with Gideon for a year, but can't say I really know him. He can be testy at times. It's a bit like walking on eggshells. Don't get me wrong, he's a good boss, and he believes in the work we're doing at Fresh Start, but..." Dalton shrugged. "At the time of Ruby's disappearance, they were working on one of our biggest fundraisers of the year. I figured the stress was getting to him and he might've taken it out on her. Gideon isn't always careful with his words."

Interesting. Eli leaned against his truck. "Who keeps track of the money coming in and out of Fresh Start?"

Dalton frowned. "Gideon's officially in charge, but I know Ruby helped him. Like I said, we get a lot of donations and bookkeeping is a tedious job. Why are you asking?"

He didn't want to explain about the money laundering. Not yet. "Do you know Jesse O'Neal?"

A shadow crossed Dalton's face. "I do. He was a member of our community but started using again a few months ago. It's not uncommon for addicts to relapse. It can take several tries before they get sober."

"He was arrested yesterday. Jesse broke into Mrs. Morales's home and attacked her. Can you think of any reason he would do that?"

Dalton's mouth dropped open in shock. "No. Jesse and Ruby barely knew each other." His brow creased. "What on earth is going on?"

"That's what we're trying to find out." Eli switched topics. "Do you know Albert Greer?"

"Not personally. I've heard some of the staff talk about him though. He used to be one of the teachers here at Fresh Start, but they had to fire him after several members complained."

"Do you know if Ruby and Albert had any interaction?"

"No. Albert was long gone by the time I was hired." He raised a finger as if a thought had just occurred to him. "I know Ruby had a problem with someone else." Dalton paused and then winced. "I'm not sure how much I should say. This person was a member."

"It won't go any further than us." Eli leveled his gaze at his brother. "We have evidence Ruby is alive and being held against her will. Anything you can tell us would be helpful. All we want is to find her."

Dalton seemed stunned by Eli's statement, but he quickly recovered. "Do you know Dallas Redding?"

The tour guide. The same man who'd been stalking Ruby.

Eli stiffened. "I know him. What happened?"

SEVENTEEN

Eli held his breath, waiting for Dalton to gather his thoughts. His brother had always been careful with his words, even as a kid. A side effect of growing up with a man who'd beat them if they so much as breathed wrong.

"Ruby complained about Dallas Redding bothering her," Dalton said. "He flirted, followed her around, asked her out on dates, that kind of thing. She'd turned him down several times, but he persisted. I intervened and told him to stay away from her. Initially, he listened, but then he cornered her in a storage closet and wouldn't let her leave until she explained why she wouldn't go out with him. Ruby was understandably frightened. I immediately consulted with Gideon and we revoked Dallas's membership."

"Did you report the incident to law enforcement?"

"Ruby insisted we keep it quiet. She didn't want to create a fuss." Dalton blew out a breath. "I disagreed with her decision but had to respect it."

"When was this?"

"About a month before she disappeared." Dalton stiffened, his complexion growing pale. "He didn't stop bothering her, did he?"

Eli shared a glance with Sienna. Maybe they'd written off Dallas too quickly. "No. He didn't." Then he clapped his brother on the shoulder. They knew firsthand what it was like to be at the mercy of someone bigger and stronger. He sensed horrible images were running through Dalton's head. The guilt would eat him alive if he let it. "It's not your fault. You did everything you could. Ruby decided not to press charges. You couldn't force her."

Dalton rubbed his eyes. "Yeah. Still..." He dropped his hand. "She's a sweet person. Is there anything else I can do to help?"

"Keep your eyes and ears open." Sienna glanced back at the converted warehouse. "Talk to some of the other staff, especially any of the women Ruby was close to. She might've told one of them what was bothering her in the days before her disappearance." She pulled out a business card. "This has my cell number on it. Call me anytime, day or night."

Dalton nodded. "I can do that." He glanced at Eli. "If you have some time to talk one day soon, I'd like to get together."

"Come to my house for dinner," Sienna interjected. "Tonight."

What was she doing? They were working a case. While Eli wanted to have a frank conversation with his brother, now wasn't the time to delve into personal issues. He barely had the emotional bandwidth to tackle his history with Sienna, and that wasn't nearly as complicated as his relationship with Dalton.

And what about the money laundering? Eli didn't want to believe his brother was involved, but right now, everyone was a suspect. He tossed Sienna a dirty look, but she ignored it. Per usual. She was on a mission, and nothing would deter her.

Dalton's lips curved upward. "I run a support group tonight, but I can come tomorrow, if that's okay."

"Tomorrow is great." Sienna hugged him enthusiastically. "Six o'clock. And come hungry. There's nothing my mom loves more than feeding people."

He laughed. "You've got a deal." Dalton released her and then extended his hand to Eli. "Good to see you, brother."

"You too." Eli clasped Dalton's hand in his before finally giving in to his urge and embracing his brother in a manly, one-armed hug. Dalton hesitated and then hugged him back. It was awkward and completely unfamiliar, but still felt right anyway.

With a last wave and a cheeky grin, Dalton disappeared back inside the building. Eli waited until he was gone before turning to Sienna. "You shouldn't have invited him to dinner."

She crossed her arms over her chest. "You're right. You should have."

"We're working a case—"

"Didn't you hear a cotton-pickin' word I said to you

yesterday?" She threw out a hand toward the building. "What about what Dalton said? He overdosed and nearly died." Her nostrils flared as she stepped closer and then jabbed a finger in his chest. "We aren't guaranteed tomorrow, Eli. Getting shot should've taught you that, but you're hardheaded so I obviously need to help you."

"Really?"

"Yes, really. Stop acting like you have all the time in the world to set things right. God has given you a precious gift. He's brought you and Dalton together again, so you can heal the hurt between you. My suggestion, not that you'll bother to listen, is that you take the opportunity."

He grabbed her wrist, halting her offending fingertip from poking him again. The woman was infuriating. She was also right. He'd allowed far too much time to pass without mending the hurt with his brother. Finding Ruby was important, but if he was being honest, it wasn't the real reason he was avoiding the necessary conversation with Dalton. "I'm scared, Sienna."

The spark of anger died in her eyes, and her rigid stance softened. "Of what?"

"I don't know." It was a confusing knot, and Eli wasn't sure he could sort it out. "There's a painful history between us. Our childhood was one big mess. I did my best to protect him but failed. He made a lot of bad choices out of pain and ended up an addict. In the end, we hurt each other and I'm not sure there's a way back from that. Some things are too broken to be fixed."

"That's not true." She flattened her hand and laid it

on his heart. "Both people have to want to repair the relationship, yes, but things can always be fixed with the grace of God." She met his gaze. "Even if Dalton didn't want to reconnect, God is the one with the power to ease the suffering in your heart. You only have to ask Him."

"Sometimes He feels far away."

"He isn't." Her gorgeous lips lifted into a smile, a mischievous twinkle in her eyes. "Sometimes our human stubbornness prevents us from listening. Know anyone like that?"

Eli kissed her nose. "Good thing I have you to help me."

She laughed. "You better believe it."

Their gazes caught and held. Eli knew he should back up, but his body refused to obey. The cold had added color to her cheeks and the waning sunlight highlighted the copper strands buried in her curls. She was stunning. Intelligent. Fierce in her faith and unapologetic about doing the right thing, no matter the cost to herself. Sienna was unlike anyone he'd ever met. She was one-of-a-kind.

Butterflies rioted his insides as her gaze dropped to his lips. He froze, barely breathing for fear of breaking the spell. He'd never wanted to kiss anyone so much before. But the choice had to be hers. She'd asked to put their relationship on ice until the case was over. Eli would abide by that commitment, especially since he'd been the one to foolishly walk away.

Inch by inch, Sienna drew closer. Kissing her wouldn't be smart. His heart was already too far gone as it was, but he wouldn't deny her. He couldn't. She was his weakness. Always had been.

Tires squealed.

The sound burst the intimate bubble surrounding them. Eli's head jerked up. A white van spun into the parking lot, the side door already open. It sped straight for them. In half a heartbeat, it screeched to a stop as three men in ski masks burst out of the vehicle.

Eli shoved Sienna behind him as something whizzed through the air. White-hot agony exploded inside him as every muscle in his body tensed all at once. The feeling was familiar. He'd experienced it once in a law enforcement training class. A Taser. Although this was far stronger than anything legally on the market. It felt like his heart was about to explode.

Sienna screamed, the sound far away, as he hit the ground. In his head, he was yelling at her to run, but the words refused to come. Her form was a blur as two men hauled her into the van. Eli tried to will his body to move, but another jolt of electricity sent him crashing back down to the pavement. He couldn't breathe.

The main door to Fresh Start opened. Dalton burst out. His baby brother, fiercely running to the rescue, with nothing but a baseball bat and foolhearted bravery.

Rough hands grabbed Eli. His wrists were quickly bound. Something heavy enveloped his head. A hood. It covered his eyes and made it hard to breathe. He sucked in desperate air, claustrophobia immediately taking hold, but only got a mouthful of fabric. His knee slammed into the edge of the van and then he was lifted inside, shoved toward the back. The door slammed shut.

In the next second, they were moving. The tires squealed again as the van flew out of the parking lot. Eli's body rolled, slamming into something soft that smelled like apples and sunshine. Sienna. His fingers found hers for the briefest moment as the true nature of their situation sank into him.

They'd been kidnapped.

And were likely being driven to their deaths.

EIGHTEEN

Sienna groaned.

Chills overtook her form, and a drum pounded inside her head in conjunction with her heartbeat. Her mouth felt like it was full of cotton. A slight rocking threatened to lull her back into the darkness, but some buried instinct inside her fought against it. She peeled her eyes open. Her vision was blurry, and it took several tries to focus.

A metal floor. She was lying on a hard icy-cold floor. Her hands were bound behind her back.

With a gasp, she sat up as the memory of the attack in the parking lot slammed into her, along with a wave of sudden fear. Nausea rolled her stomach. Bile burned the back of her throat and her vision blurred again. Sienna slammed her eyes shut to regain her equilibrium. She'd been drugged. After the masked men grabbed her and threw her into the van, they'd injected her with something.

Slowly. She needed to take things slowly.

Once her stomach settled, Sienna opened her eyes again. The scent of saltwater, fish, and gasoline filled her nose. The room was small with a metal floor and metal walls. A ship? Some kind of commercial vessel, bigger than Albert's, but still used for fishing. She was in a cabin. A bed, a small table, and a chair were bolted to the floor.

Where was Eli? The last thing she remembered was seeing him hit the ground after he'd been Tased. Had the masked men kidnapped him too? Or only her? Fear gripped her insides as she envisioned Eli shot and killed after being incapacitated. Her heart raced as dizziness swept over her. Tears pricked her eyes.

No. It took everything inside Sienna to wrestle her runaway emotions back under control. She couldn't envision the worst. Survival meant keeping her mind focused on the most immediate problem. Right now, that was getting free of these binds and finding a way out of this room.

She twisted her hands, letting her fingers trace the restraints encircling her wrists. Zip ties. Breaking them, even with her wrists bound behind her back was possible, but she needed to stand.

Using the wall as leverage, Sienna struggled to a standing position. Her head swam as the drugs coursing through her system continued to wreak havoc on her senses. Black dots danced at the edges of her vision. She planted her gaze on a notch in the floor and focused on breathing in through her nose and out through her mouth until the dizziness faded.

A lock snicked and the door to the cabin flew open. Eli's familiar form appeared. Relief surged inside Sienna, but it was short-lived. His face was bruised and bloody, as if he'd been beaten.

Eli flew inside the cabin, knocked off his feet by a force from behind. He slammed into the unyielding metal floor with a bone-jarring sound that instinctively caused Sienna to wince. She dropped to her knees beside him. "Eli!"

"I'm okay, babe." He struggled to sit up, but it was difficult to do with his hands tied behind his back.

A shadow fell over them.

Sienna's heart raced as her gaze lifted to their captor. The man had a bulky build with a square face and bushy brows over beady eyes. His sneer sent ice through her veins even as recognition zipped through her. Luis Greer. Albert's cousin.

"Have you lost your mind?" The words came out piping hot as fury at their kidnapping and Eli's beating replaced the fear. And her better common sense. Sienna helped Eli into a seated position. "He's a Texas Ranger. Every law enforcement agency in the state will hunt you down if you don't let us go."

Luis's sneer only widened. "You think I care? I've already got the Houston Police Department on my tail. The cops don't scare me." He stepped forward and grabbed her arm, yanking her into a standing position.

The hatred pouring from him was palpable. "You killed my cousin."

She met his heated gaze, refusing to let him see the terror streaking through him. "No, I didn't. Albert was murdered by someone else before I got there."

He punched her in the stomach. Fiery heat bellowed from her belly, stealing her breath. Her eyes watered. She collapsed onto the cold metal floor. Eli hollered but got a boot in his own stomach for the trouble.

Luis's laugh cut through their wheezing. "You two are pathetic." He glanced behind him at the man standing in the doorway. His brother, Tony. "Keep an eye on them. Once we get word from the boss, we'll finish this once and for all."

Tony scratched at his crooked nose. His chubby cheeks and soft chin gave him a youthful appearance, but his eyes were just as mean as his brother's. "I don't understand why we don't kill them now."

"The boss wants to question them. We need to know how much the police have figured out before the shipment is ready. Otherwise everything goes south." Luis grinned, like a cat that ate the canary. "I doubt they'll talk willingly, so we'll have to convince them."

Sienna was going to throw up. The Greer brothers were talking about torturing them as if they were deciding where to go on vacation. She didn't understand everything that was going on, but two things were obvious. First, the Greer brothers were taking orders from someone. And second, they needed to get off this boat before the boss arrived, whoever he was.

It was a desperate situation, and she wasn't sure how they could manage it. *Please God, we need Your help.*

Luis punched his brother in the shoulder. "Don't get distracted. These two aren't like that other chick. They'll cause trouble if you don't keep watch."

Other chick? Ruby? Sienna sucked in a breath. "Where's Ruby?"

Tony scowled. "She ain't here, so stop bellowing before I cut your tongue out." He turned back to his brother. "Go. I've got this."

Luis nodded and then left, closing the door behind him but not locking it. Eli struggled into a sitting position with Sienna's help. Up close, his wounds looked even worse, and judging from the pain creasing his features, the beating extended beyond his face.

He sagged against the wall. His gaze swept over her. "You hurt?"

"No." Her heart clenched. Eli was in this mess because of her. He'd come back to Sandalwood to bail her out of trouble and then refused to leave even when things became increasingly dangerous. He was a fighter. This was the man she'd fallen in love with all those years ago. The one she'd thought would never leave her. How had things between them gone so wrong?

They were both to blame. Yes, Eli had walked away from their relationship, but she'd intervened against his wishes. Sienna should've fought harder to get him to listen to her. Instead, she'd insisted on doing it her way. Eli hadn't been wrong about that.

Despite all of their mistakes, the love was still there.

The truth of that was inescapable, and Sienna wanted a second chance with him. It was a risk, yes, but she didn't live her life in half-measures. And Eli was worth it. If they got out of this, she intended to tell him as much.

No, not if. When.

Sienna leaned closer to Eli so Tony wouldn't overhear their conversation. "How badly are you hurt?"

Eli glared at the pacing man on the other side of the room. "I can take him." His voice was hushed but loaded with rage. And determination.

Good. They would need both.

Sienna tore her gaze away from Eli and focused on Tony. The criminal held a gun in one hand and a cell phone in the other. He leaned his bulky weight against the small table. He tapped the cell phone screen with a pudgy thumb. Then his face screwed up with annoyance. Of the two Greer brothers, Tony was the weaker link. He was the muscle of the operation and not the brains. They simply needed an opening.

Sienna tried to maneuver her hands out of the zip ties, but they were too tight. She winced as the edge of the binds cut her skin. Blood seeped from the wound. It dripped off her fingers. No good. Change of plan. She felt along the wall for any rough edge to cut the tie off with, but that was a dead end too.

Tony lifted his phone toward the ceiling and huffed. His annoyance was growing. No signal? Impatience could work in their favor.

Sienna leaned against Eli. "Make yourself look weak. Sag against me."

He shot her a questioning look but did as she said. The weight of his body against hers was comforting. Sienna did her best to look weak and tired as well. It didn't take much effort. The drugs were still looping in her system, and now that the adrenaline was wearing off, sleep was beckoning.

With every passing moment, Tony grew more restless. He attempted to get a signal from various points in the room, but nothing worked. Finally, he glanced in their direction, debated something in his head for a long moment, and then snarled. "I'm stepping out for a moment, but I'm locking you inside here. You make so much as a peep, and I shoot you the minute I come back."

Internally, Sienna was doing a happy dance, but she didn't allow a flicker of that emotion to leech onto her face. Instead, she stifled a sob as if terrified. "Please let us go."

"Oh, shut up." Tony marched to the door. Without another word, he slipped out, the bolt driving home behind him. His footsteps pounded against the metal floor as he moved away from the room, presumably to a place with better Wi-Fi.

Eli shook his head. "Unbelievable. How did you know he'd leave us in here?"

"Watching prisoners gets boring." Sienna struggled to her feet. "He's probably downloading a show on his phone right now. We have to hurry."

She bent over slightly at the waist and raised her bound arms higher behind her back before bringing them down sharply against her rear end. The zip ties didn't break. Her heart rate increased as she attempted the move again.

This time, the ties snapped. Sienna turned toward Eli with a triumphant grin. "Those YouTube videos I watched came in handy after all."

He chuckled and then winced. "Don't make me laugh." Eli mirrored her trick and his own binds snapped off.

The sound of footsteps coming toward the room sent Sienna's heart rate into overdrive. They didn't have a game plan yet. Her gaze swept the room for some kind of weapon. Nothing.

Eli lifted a finger to his lips and then pushed her toward the wall behind the door. When Tony opened it, he wouldn't see them.

The metal was cold against her back. Sienna shivered with fear as the footsteps grew louder. Eli held out a hand to indicate she should wait. Then he turned and leaned forward on the balls of his feet in preparation to tackle Tony when he entered the room.

It was a desperate move, but it was the only one they had.

The lock clicked open. Sienna sent up a silent prayer. Her breath caught in her chest and her pulse roared in her ears.

The door swung inward.

NINETEEN

The only thing Eli had going for him was the element of surprise and his fierce need to protect Sienna.

No one would hurt her. Not while there was breath in his body.

Tony entered the cabin, his gaze locked on his phone screen. Eli waited until he was clear of the door and then launched himself at the thug. They crashed to a heap on the metal floor. The cell phone went flying across the room, but Tony maintained his hold on the gun. He reared up to pistol-whip Eli, but his position on the ground made the move difficult.

Adrenaline pulsed through Eli's veins as he deflected the hit and punched Tony in the throat. The man gagged. His face turned red.

Eli didn't wait. He followed up the hit with another to the chin. Pain sang up his arm, but he barely felt it. He grabbed the gun in Tony's hand, but the criminal wouldn't let go. Eli smashed Tony's hand against the unyielding floor.

A wild punch made contact with Eli's ribs. He hissed as agony shot straight through his body. The beating he'd taken earlier after arriving on the ship hadn't been the worst of his life, but it'd left him with serious bruises. Still he didn't release Tony's hand. A childhood of abuse had taught Eli how to block out the pain. He smashed the gunman's hand against the hard floor. If they didn't disarm Tony, there was no chance for survival.

Finally, with a third hit, the gun clattered to the floor. Tony's face was beat red, and he appeared on the verge of passing out. The punch to the throat, combined with Eli's body weight crushing his lungs, had robbed him of air. Eli shoved the gun away just as Tony's eyes rolled back into his head. He went limp.

Sienna appeared by Eli's side. "Is he dead?"

"Unconscious." He'd passed out from a lack of oxygen. Tony would wake up with a terrible headache, but he'd live. Eli flipped the man over and grabbed his wrists. "Find something to tie him up with."

"Already did."

She handed him a length of rope. The drawers underneath the bed hung open, and Eli realized she'd been searching for something to use since Tony entered the room. He tied the criminal's hands together using knots he'd perfected while tending Ryker's family ranch as a teen.

Sienna brought more rope. "We can tie him to the

table. I didn't find anything to put over his mouth though. Once he wakes up, he'll start screaming."

"Then we need to be off this boat before that happens."

Eli dragged the unconscious man's body across the floor and secured him to the table bolted to the floor. Once he was certain Tony wouldn't go anywhere anytime soon, he scooped up the handgun from the floor. A Smith & Wesson. He'd shot one before. Eli popped out the magazine and checked the bullets before slamming it back home. Fifteen rounds. He prayed they wouldn't need them. Then he grabbed Sienna's hand. "Let's go."

A quick check of the hall revealed it was empty. Eli's heart thundered against his rib cage as they exited the room, closing the door behind them. He loathed to let go of Sienna's hand, but it would be easier to maneuver, and if necessary, shoot, if she was behind him. "Hold on to my belt and stay with me."

She gave a sharp nod. Then her fingers threaded through the rear loop on his jeans. No questions. No discussion. Sheer trust. It wasn't a small matter. Sienna was as independent as they came. She was used to calling the shots and trusting her own instincts above anything else. That she so willingly allowed him to take the lead in this perilous and unknown situation touched Eli in ways he couldn't begin to process.

Please God, help me get Sienna out of here. Guide my steps.

The prayer centered him. Eli traversed the hallway

on silent feet, Sienna close enough to his back, he felt her breath on his neck. It'd been a mistake for the Greer brothers to escort him through the ship from the helm to the cabin. Eli had gotten a good look at the vessel. He knew the layout.

He'd also seen a small dingy tied to the stern. It didn't feel like the ship was moving, which meant they were still close to shore. But there were several criminals on board. They had to make it across the ship without being seen before Tony woke up.

Cold air caressed his overheated skin as Eli slipped onto the deck. Sienna followed, sticking to the shadows without being told. It was pitch-black outside. Clouds hid the moon and stars. Drizzle peppered Eli's clothes, and the deck was slick with rainwater. Only an hour ago, it'd been light enough to see. Once again, he gave thanks to God. It felt strange to be grateful for the beating he'd taken, but if Eli had been locked below deck with Sienna, he wouldn't have known about the dingy.

Voices filtered from the bridge of the ship. That's probably where Luis had gone.

Eli quietly slipped deeper into the shadows, bringing Sienna with him. He resisted the urge to break into a sprint. Someone could be paroling the deck. It was wiser to move cautiously.

As if his thoughts caused someone to materialize, a thug wearing a heavy coat and thick glasses came around the corner. The man carried an assault rifle.

Eli directed Sienna behind a crane used to haul fishing nets from the ocean. Footsteps grew louder as the man neared. Sienna's body pressed against Eli's. She felt so small and fragile. Fear caused her to tremble.

Eli held his weapon at the ready. Adrenaline threatened to narrow his focus. He forced a breath. Then another. The criminal stopped in front of their hiding spot. Eli's heart pounded so loudly against his rib cage, he was certain the man could hear it. What was he doing? Had he spotted them?

The sound of a match striking flint proceeded a flare of light. Eli didn't move. Every cell of his body was fixed on calculating options should things go badly. A second later, the match hit the ground and was smashed under the criminal's boot. The stench of a cigarette floated on the breeze as he moved away, whistling, to the port side of the ship.

Eli breathed out. That'd been close. Too close.

He leaned over to whisper in Sienna's ear. The scent of apples and sunshine filled his senses and his chest constricted. Losing her wasn't an option. She was a part of him. As angry as Eli had been with her, he'd never stopped loving her. "There's a dingy attached to the stern. If we get caught, I want you to run. Don't look back, don't wait for me. You get off this ship, you understand me?"

She pulled back just enough to face him. Her features were shrouded in darkness. Then she moved closer and pressed her lips softly to his. A brief kiss, nothing more than a brush of their mouths, but it sent Eli's heart rate into the stratosphere.

"We're a team, Eli, and we're getting off this boat

together."

Her voice was hushed, but the thread of determination running through it was evident. The stubborn woman. She wouldn't leave him, even if it meant saving herself. He wasn't surprised by her answer. Once again, Eli was struck with the notion that he'd made a foolish mistake in walking away from her. How could he have ever believed she'd betray him? Maybe he was more like his abusive father than he wanted to admit. Self-righteous. Cynical. Distrusting.

It was a bitter pill to swallow. He didn't want to be the kind of man who turned his back on loved ones. But actions spoke for themselves. He was that kind of man.

It needed to change. And it would. Starting now.

Eli kissed Sienna quickly once more and then he peered around the collection of nets they were hiding behind. The coast was clear. "Let's move."

Once again, Sienna hung onto his belt as they shifted in the shadows toward the rear of the boat. Damp rain and salty air mingled together, collecting on Eli's eyelashes and chilling his skin. His senses were attuned to anyone heading their direction. Thankfully, they reached the stern without running into any more guards.

The shore was nothing more than a dark hulk, faintly visible in the dark. An inflatable raft with a motor floated in the black water. It was attached to the ship with two ropes. The only way into it was by climbing a rickety ladder.

He didn't want to send Sienna down first. Not without testing the strength of the ladder, but there was no time for normal safety measures. Eli turned to her. "Go down first. Start the motor if you can. I'll cover you and then untie the ropes attaching it to the ship."

"Don't get shot."

He grinned, despite the danger they were in. "I don't plan on it."

She hooked a leg over the side of the boat and then scaled down the ladder like a spider monkey. Eli breathed a sigh of relief once she was in the raft. He yanked on the first rope securing the dingy to the fishing vessel, and the knot unfurled with ease.

A shout came from the other side of the ship. Eli's heart rate skyrocketed. They'd been discovered.

He ran to the other rope and gave it a yank as the sound of boots thundered on the deck, followed by more yells. They had seconds. Maybe.

The motor in the raft sputtered, but then died. Eli hooked his leg over the edge of the boat as several men carrying rifles rounded the corner. He caught a glimpse of Luis's face before scrambling down the ladder. The man was furious. Out for blood. If he caught them again, they wouldn't survive.

Bullets burst from the rifles. Eli jumped the last few rungs of the ladder and landed in the boat. The motor sputtered to life. The raft shot forward, knocking him off his feet. He tipped over, bouncing off the inflatable surface, and then scrambled toward Sienna. He used his body to cover hers, his hand helping to steer the raft toward shore, as the gunmen reached the edge of the fishing vessel.

They weren't out of range of those rifles. Not yet.

Gunfire erupted.

TWENTY

They escaped by the grace of God.

The next morning, every muscle in Eli's body hurt. That didn't prevent him from arriving at the Sandalwood Police Department, Sienna at his side, to join his teammates in breaking down what they knew about the case so far.

He was surprised to see Chief Ramirez already in the conference room. The lawman was seated at the head of the table. On his left was Eli's boss, Lieutenant Rodriguez. Her dark hair was tied back into a tight ponytail, her skin clear of any makeup. She rose to greet them.

"I'm glad to see you're in one piece." She shook Eli's hand, a smile lifting her lips. "If I were you, I'd call the doctor and explain that in the past five days, you've been shot at, kidnapped, escaped from a boat, and been in two fist fights. Surely he can clear you for active duty."

Eli chuckled and then smothered a wince as his

cracked rib protested the movement. "Not once he gets a look at my fresh bruises."

The emergency room doctor had advised him to take it easy for the next few days. Fat chance of that happening. But he was encouraged that his boss was anxious for his return to active duty. Eli hoped that meant the chief wouldn't file an official complaint about his continued involvement in the case.

Vikki turned to Sienna and extended her hand. "It's a pleasure to finally meet you, Ms. Evans. Your reputation precedes you."

"Sienna, please." She raised her brows, glancing toward the chief. "As for my reputation, I can only imagine the things you've heard."

"I'll admit, it hasn't all been good." The chief rose and joined them. His uniform was wrinkled and bags drooped under his eyes. It didn't appear he'd slept at all in the last few days. "But I'm man enough to admit when I was wrong. Both of you tried to tell me over and over again that Ruby's disappearance was connected to Albert's murder and the attacks on y'all. I refused to listen, and that was a grave mistake that nearly cost you both your lives. I owe you an apology, Sienna." He locked eyes with Eli. "You too, Ranger Goodwin."

Eli struggled but managed to keep his jaw from falling open. He'd hoped the chief would eventually come around, but didn't allow himself to believe it would truly happen. "Does this mean you're going to drop the charges against Sienna?"

"I am."

Relief flooded over Eli with the swiftness of a tsunami. He wanted to whoop with joy, but held himself back. Instead, he reached for Sienna's hand and gave it a squeeze. It wasn't over. They still had killers to catch and Ruby to find, but this was a major victory.

Sienna appeared stunned but quickly recovered. She interlaced her fingers with Eli and squeezed his hand back before turning her attention to the chief. "Thank you, sir."

"No need to thank me for doing the right thing."

"Maybe not, but you were right about the Greer brothers' involvement. I should have taken you more seriously about that." She blew out a breath. "Can we finally bury the hatchet between us? Neither of us is going anywhere and I think we'll be more successful working together than against one another."

The chief hesitated and then extended his hand toward her. "It's buried and done."

They shook hands, sealing the deal, just as the conference room door opened. Cole and Ryker poured in. The scent of coffee and warm bread wafted from the takeaway items in their hands. Both rangers wore the same clothes they'd had on yesterday. Cole's hair was rumpled and his boots muddy. Ryker sported a day's growth of whiskers on his chin and cheeks.

"Morning." Cole lifted the bag in his hands. "We brought breakfast. Hope everyone likes kolaches."

The next few minutes were spent doling out coffees and organizing the food. Eli scarfed down his first kolache in five bites. He hadn't eaten much since the escape from the boat and was suddenly starving. Stress often messed with his stomach. Knowing that the police chief and the rangers were now on the same page, plus the charges being dropped against Sienna, had lifted some of the weight crushing his shoulders. For the first time since arriving in Sandalwood, Eli felt like part of a team again. He'd missed it.

Ryker, Sienna, Chief Ramirez, and Lieutenant Rodriguez were on the far side of the room chatting. Sienna laughed at something Ryker said, and Eli's gaze was drawn to her. She was amazing. Less than twenty-four hours ago, they'd been held hostage by gun-wielding thugs, but she hadn't let that stop her from doing everything to find Ruby. Including making peace with the police chief.

He was falling in love with her.

No, that wasn't right. If Eli was honest with himself, he'd never stopped loving Sienna.

But could they make a new relationship work? Would she forgive him for walking away five years ago?

He didn't know the answer to those questions. There hadn't been time to discuss their relationship since the attack. They'd gotten to shore, called the authorities, and been taken straight to the hospital. After being checked out, they were released, but it was well after midnight and both of them were exhausted. They'd gotten up early for this morning's meeting.

Cole snagged the chair next to Eli and handed him another kolache. "How are you feeling?"

He accepted the offering, biting into the soft bread.

Melted cheese and fragrant sausage exploded on his tongue. "Better than yesterday."

His friend nodded, but Eli sensed Cole needed to say something. He set his kolache down. "Everything okay?"

"I don't know." Cole jerked his chin toward Ryker. "A few days ago, our friend over there gave me a dressing down. He said it appeared I was taking the chief's side over yours. You should know that's not the case. I was worried about you. And your career. It looked like you were throwing everything away for Sienna and..." He sighed. "I didn't want to see you get hurt."

Eli was touched by the explanation. He also understood the difficult position Cole had been placed in. "There are no hard feelings on my side." He clapped Cole on the shoulder. "You were looking out for me. That's what friends do for each other."

The tension in Cole's posture loosened. His expression grew determined. "We're gonna get these guys."

Eli nodded. "Yeah, we are."

Lieutenant Rodriguez clapped her hands and gestured for everyone to take a seat. Sienna slipped into the chair on the other side of Eli. Ryker sat across from them and the chief claimed his spot at the head of the table. Immediately, everyone in the room shifted into work mode.

"Here's what we know so far," Vikki said. "The fishing vessel Eli and Sienna were held captive on has been identified as The Trident IV. It's registered in Panama and owned by a Panama corporation named Successful Fishermen."

"Can we identify the owners of the company?"

"No. Under Panama legislation, the shareholders of a corporation are shielded. We're working to obtain a warrant to gain access to the formation documents, but that's going to take a while. Currently, the Coast Guard is searching for the vessel, but it hasn't been found yet."

"If they're smart, they went back to Panama." Sienna frowned. "Tony and Luis discussed a shipment coming in. Do we have any idea what they were referring to?"

"Drugs." Cole leaned back in his chair, twirling a pen between his fingers like a baton. "We've long suspected the Greer brothers are responsible for much of the Oxycontin, heroine, and cocaine in this area. My guess is, they're smuggling the drugs in from South America using The Trident IV. Then they have a system of dealers they use to distribute the goods across several counties."

Eli nodded as some pieces of the puzzle started snapping into place. "If that's so, they're getting a lot of illegal funds and need to launder the money. Which is where Fresh Start comes in."

"Yep." Ryker selected another kolache from the box. "I checked out the invoices Ruby had saved in the secret file on her computer. Some of them are fake companies. Others are real, but they exist only on paper. We're working on obtaining the real names of the shareholders, but it'll take a bit more time."

It was all making more sense. Eli leaned forward, resting his elbows on the table. "Ruby was working for Fresh Start. She figures out the charity is laundering money and isn't sure what to do about it. Ruby either confides in someone or her investigation is discovered. She's kidnapped." Eli remembered Tony and Luis talking on the ship. "I think the Greer brothers nabbed her. Why she wasn't killed right away, I can't say, but they kept her alive long enough Ruby was able to make a desperate call to her grandmother."

"She was trying to tell her about the secret file on her computer," Sienna filled in. "But her grandmother didn't understand what Ruby was saying. That's why we didn't find the file until after Jesse broke in."

Eli nodded. "Albert knew his cousins had kidnapped Ruby. He also knew who his cousins were working for. He needs cash, and in a desperate ploy to get some, blackmails his cousins' boss. The move backfires, because the boss kills him, framing Sienna for the murder in the hopes it'll get rid of two problems at the same time. Albert and Sienna."

"Except it didn't stop the investigation. So he switches to trying to kill me. He also hires Jesse to break into Ruby's house to steal her computer."

"Jesse." Eli sat up straight in his chair. "He was either hired by the Greer brothers or hired by their boss. Either way, he could know more than we realize."

"He's in the wind." Chief Ramirez scraped a hand through his hair. "Jesse made bond yesterday, and no one has seen him since. I've put out a be-on-the-lookout and named him as a person of interest, but so far, law enforcement hasn't found him."

Eli winced. "He may not be alive anymore." It was a chilling thought but a realistic one. So far, the Greer brothers and their boss had kidnapped one woman, killed Albert, and attempted to murder Sienna and Eli several times. "The Greer brothers believe Sienna is responsible for Albert's death. They said as much on the ship. So whoever their boss is, he's not telling them the truth about their cousin's death."

"Smart." Cole kept twirling his pen. "I'm sure the Greer brothers would turn on him if they knew he killed their cousin."

"The real question is," Sienna said. "Who are the Greer brothers working for? It has to be someone at Fresh Start. Everything keeps coming back to that place."

"I've known Gideon Wade since he was a toddler." Chief Ramirez's mouth thinned into a flat line. "Several members of the Wade family have fallen into addiction. It's affected him greatly. He's dedicated to making Fresh Start a success and the work that charity has done for this community can't be measured. He's not laundering money for the Greer brothers. I can assure you of that."

Eli appreciated the chief's loyalty, but that wasn't evidence. "Have we done a thorough background check on Gideon?"

"It's in progress." Ryker lifted a shoulder. "At this moment, everything appears to be on the up and up. Gideon's never been arrested, and he's living within his means." He hesitated. "I interviewed several members of the Fresh Start staff. In order to launder the money, the individual would need access to the invoices, the donations that came in, and the business bank accounts. There are only three people with that kind of access. Gideon, Ruby, and..."

Ryker shifted uncomfortably.

Eli met his gaze. He already knew what his friend was about to say. The food and coffee congealed in his stomach, and for a moment, he was about to throw up. He swallowed hard. "The other person with access is my brother, Dalton, isn't it?"

"Yes."

TWENTY-ONE

Sienna shut her hymnal as the Sunday afternoon service came to a close. The smell of fresh flowers decorating the main aisle and the altar were a stark contrast to the bitter weather outside. It was still raining with no sign of letting up. There were flash flood warnings for the county. Another thing working against law enforcement's search for Ruby and Jesse. The weather also prevented the Coast Guard from scouring the nearby waters for the Trident IV.

Parishioners began leaving. Few people had braved the horrible weather to attend the service. Since Sienna and Eli were already in town for the meeting at the police station, it'd been a quick five-minute drive to the church. Prayer was all they could offer. Chief Ramirez and Lieutenant Rodriguez requested Sienna and Eli remove themselves from the investigation now that the rangers and the Sandalwood Police Department were working together.

Their request was logical, especially since Dalton

was a suspect. It wasn't easy for Sienna to take a step back, but she'd do whatever was necessary to help find Ruby.

She returned the hymnal to its place at the end of the pew before reclaiming her seat next to Eli. His head was bowed in prayer. Sienna's heart cracked when he finished and the glitter of tears sparkled in his sky blue eyes. She threaded an arm through his and rested her head on his shoulder. "Are you thinking about canceling our dinner with Dalton tonight?"

He took her hand in both of his, his fingers absently playing with the cross bracelet dangling from her wrist. "No. I spoke with Ryker and Cole about it. We decided canceling might tip Dalton off. It's better if he doesn't know we're investigating him."

"Are you going to question him about the money laundering?"

"No. Again, we don't want to tip him off." He sighed. "It won't be easy, but I'm determined to do what's necessary to keep the case on track. Besides, there are things I need to say to Dalton and they're true whether he's involved in this mess or not."

"Do you really believe he's behind this?" Sienna frowned. "He ran out of Fresh Start carrying a bat, prepared to fight off the kidnappers. Why would he do that if he was the one who'd ordered it?"

"To make himself look innocent. There were cameras in the parking lot of Fresh Start. Dalton running to our rescue makes it less likely law enforcement would believe he's involved in the criminal activity happening at the charity. It wouldn't be the first time a criminal has done that. Murderers will often volunteer on search-and-rescue teams to help find their victims, for example. There's something about being close to the investigation that feeds their arrogance."

"Dalton never struck me as arrogant. Too smart for his own good, yes. Destructive, yes. But not arrogant."

"I agree, but we're also too close to the situation to see it clearly. There's a reason why law enforcement isn't supposed to work cases involving family members. We're biased. Ryker and Cole will get to the bottom of it though. I trust them." He turned and brushed a kiss across her forehead. "Thank you for suggesting we come to church service. I needed it more than I realized."

"So did I. It's been a rough week."

He snorted. "You can say that again." Eli was quiet for a long moment. "Do you mind if we stay for a bit and talk? There are some things I need to say."

"Of course not. What's on your mind?"

"Us."

She stiffened, surprised by his answer, and pulled back to look him in the face. A painful bruise highlighted his cheekbone and his lower lip was still swollen from yesterday's fight. He had more cuts and bruises along his arms and his posture was off-center thanks to a cracked rib. She imagined he was in pain, but in true Eli fashion, he didn't complain.

Eli studied her hand, still clasped within his, as if it held the secrets to his life. He trailed a thumb over her knuckle. The gentle touch sent a wave of warmth through her and Sienna's heart began to pound. There was so much she wanted to say, but didn't know if now was the right time. Tonight's dinner with Dalton would be stressful and Eli had never been very good at processing his emotions.

"I'm not going anywhere, Eli. This can wait until after the case is over."

"No, it can't." He turned to face her. The look in his eyes stole her breath. "We nearly died yesterday, and I made a promise on that boat that if we got off alive, I was going to be honest about how I felt. I love you, Sienna. I've always loved you. It was a mistake to walk away from our relationship five years ago and I'm so sorry for the pain I caused you."

She shook her head. "No more apologies. We both made mistakes." Now that the conversation was happening, Sienna wouldn't shy away from confessing her own errors in judgment. "Bailing Dalton out of jail against your wishes was wrong. Instead, I should've been honest with you about what I was feeling and thinking."

"You tried—"

"Not hard enough. You're stubborn, Eli. I knew that. One conversation is never enough when it comes to something you're resistant to. I should've done more. Talked more. Instead, I gave up and did things my way because I believed I was right." It felt good to say the words out loud. "We failed each other by not acting as a team."

Eli cupped her cheek. His palm was warm and it sent

a shiver through her. "I can't be your friend, Sienna. I want more than that."

"So do I..." She bit her lip. Part of her wanted to throw caution to the wind and fling herself in his arms, but another part of her knew that would be a mistake. She'd made a vow to be honest with her feelings and that started now. "Things can't go back to the way they were. Our relationship will hit hard times, and if we can't work together, then we're doomed for failure."

They'd been working as a team on Ruby's case, but only by shoving difficult conversations aside. That wasn't how real life worked. They had to be able to communicate. Sienna would fight harder to get Eli to see her point of view, but he had to be willing to listen.

"We both have to make changes. I promise to stop making unilateral decisions, but I need you to hear me out, Eli, especially when you don't like what I'm saying." Her chin trembled. "And you can't walk away again. If I give you my heart, then you have to stay and fight for us."

He swiped at the tear that fell from her lashes. "You're worth fighting for, Sienna. Our relationship is worth fighting for." Eli let out a long breath. "Yesterday, I realized that I'm more like my father than I thought. But I don't want to be that person anymore. I prayed, asking for God's guidance. Then one of the readings in today's service spoke directly to my heart as if it was meant for me."

Eli released her to reach for the program and opened it to the first page. He read the verse aloud. "Be kind and compassionate with each other, forgiving each other, just as in Christ God forgives you."

Sienna knew the verse well. It was one of her favorites.

"I haven't been living according to my faith." Eli closed the program. "I didn't approach Dalton's addiction with kindness and compassion. I was angry." He let go of a long breath. "And when you bailed him out of jail, instead of approaching you with kindness and compassion, I was angry. I've been angry, Sienna. For a long time. Since childhood. I've buried it under a mountain of responsible choices, but it's still there and it's caused me to act in ways I don't like."

The recrimination in his voice was more than she could bear. Sienna said softly. "You weren't angry. You were hurting."

He paused and then nodded. "Yes, I was." Eli lifted his gaze to hers. "But I don't want to mask my hurt with anger anymore. I'm putting my faith in God, and next time we hit rough waters, I promise to treat you with kindness and compassion. I know it's hard to believe now. It'll take time to prove it to you, but I'd like the opportunity." Eli lifted his hand and brushed away a lock of hair from her forehead. "Things will be different between us because I'm different."

"So am I." Sienna leaned in and brushed a kiss across his lips. She wanted more, but they were in a church and it wasn't appropriate. Still, the gentle touch set off a riot of butterflies in her stomach.

A bang from the rear of the church interrupted their

private moment. Sienna immediately stiffened and glanced in that direction, just as Eli half-rose from his seat, his hand reaching for his concealed weapon.

A man in a raincoat stood in the entryway. He tossed his hood back.

Dallas Redding.

Shock ran through Sienna. She hadn't seen Dallas since that day at the marina when he helped them out of the water. Did he attend church here? She'd never seen him before, although it was possible they just went to different services. She normally attended on Sunday morning.

Eli relaxed his stance, and together, they intercepted Dallas.

Sienna offered him a smile. "You missed service."

His cheeks heated. "I'm not here for service. I recognized Eli's truck in the parking lot and was hoping to catch you guys. Is there any progress on locating Ruby?" His gaze skittered away. "I've been thinking about her a lot since we talked. Her picture is all over the news, but no one seems to have any information."

Unease tripped down Sienna's spine. The last time they talked, Dallas claimed to barely know Ruby. Now he was concerned with her whereabouts. "I thought you and Ruby weren't close."

"We didn't hit it off romantically, but talk around town is that she didn't run off after all. Someone might've kidnapped her." He shuddered. "Ruby's a sweet girl. I hate to think of her at the mercy of some predator."

Sienna wasn't sure what to make of Dallas's mood

shift. Maybe he'd been flippant when talking to them at the marina but thought better of it now. His concern appeared genuine, but she couldn't ignore the way Ruby's friends talked about him. Nor could she dismiss the story Dalton told them about Dallas trapping Ruby in the supply closet at Fresh Start.

Then again, if Dalton was laundering money through the charity, he might've lied about Dallas in order to muddy the waters. Sienna's head hurt thinking about the complexity of the case. Layers and manipulations, smoke and mirrors. It was hard to know who to trust.

"The police are doing everything they can to find her." Eli rocked back on his heels. "Did you and Ruby meet at Fresh Start?"

"No. I volunteered there for a while, but quit when the season got busy. Why?"

"Curious. I heard a rumor there was an incident between you and Ruby in a supply closet. Some kind of altercation."

Dallas's brows arched in surprise. "I have no idea what you're talking about. Ruby and I barely crossed paths at Fresh Start. She handled the administrative stuff for Gideon Wade, the director, and I was teaching a course on entrepreneurship." He frowned. "Who told you there was a fight between me and Ruby?"

"It's just something we heard. Nothing to worry about if it's not true." Eli was quick to mollify him. "What did you think of Gideon Wade?"

Dallas shrugged. "He's all right. Better than most." His gaze narrowed. "Why are you asking all these questions about Fresh Start? Does Ruby's disappearance have something to do with the charity?"

"Right now, we're pursuing all leads." Eli laid a hand on the small of Sienna's back. "We'd better head out before the rain picks up again. Nice to see you, Dallas."

"You too. Drive carefully."

Sienna let Eli lead her to the main doors of the church. She glanced over her shoulder before stepping out into the cold. Dallas had shed his jacket and was sitting in one of the pews. Their interaction had left her with an unsettled feeling. "Did you get the sense he was pumping us for information?"

Eli settled his cowboy hat on his head and turned up the collar on his jacket. "Yep. But why? Simply curiosity? Or something else?"

"I don't know."

Sienna hurried across the parking lot to the truck. She slid into the passenger seat and tossed her wet hair out of her eyes. Through the droplets on the windshield, she spotted Dallas coming out of the church. He stood on the sidewalk, hood up to ward off the rain, and watched them.

The sight of him standing there, staring, chilled Sienna right to the bone.

TWENTY-TWO

Hours later, Eli stepped onto the front porch as his brother's dented sedan traversed the long driveway to the main house. A stiff wind whistled down his collar. Goosebumps rose on the back of his neck. The rain had lessened to a steady drizzle, but more thunderstorms were coming. Lightning flashed in the distance. Eli did his best to tamp down on the nerves tightening his muscles, but it wasn't easy. Before this morning's meeting at the police department, he'd been looking forward to this dinner.

Now... he wasn't sure. There were things that needed to be said, but the cloud of suspicion hanging over Dalton would color their interaction. Could his brother be part of a criminal network of drug dealers and illegal money laundering? It was a far cry from doing drugs and stealing Eli's truck, but it'd been five years since they saw each other last. A lot had changed.

Dalton parked and hopped out of the sedan, racing to the porch steps on long strides without an umbrella.

Droplets sprinkled his jacket and clung to the thick strands of his hair. He carried a set of flowers and a pie box in his hands. "This rain just won't stop."

"Tomorrow it'll get better." Eli took the dessert from his brother. The box sported Nelson's Diner in bold letters, and based on the address stamped below the restaurant name, was two counties away. "Wow. Did you drive to Knoxville for this?"

"Best cherry pie in Texas." Dalton grinned, his boyish dimple flashing. "You won't be disappointed."

Cherry pie was one of Eli's favorite desserts. The touching gestures sent a wave of familiar warmth through him. Without thinking, he lightly punched Dalton on the shoulder, falling into old habits from their childhood days. "Thanks, bro. You didn't have to go to all that trouble."

"Oh, it's not for you." His grin widened. "Sienna's mom loves cherry pie. Since she's cooking the meal, I figured it was the right thing to do."

Eli's mouth dropped open. "I was kidnapped yesterday. Surely that earns me a cherry pie."

Dalton shrugged. "Not so much. It's kinda in your job description."

"Trust me, being kidnapped is *not* in my job description."

They both laughed. Dalton had called several times, last night and this morning. The conversations were brief and slightly awkward, but like the pie, Eli was touched his brother had reached out to check on him. He desperately wanted to believe that Dalton's actions were genuine, but there was a tiny part of his brain that warned him his younger brother could be manipulating all of them. He certainly had the brains for it.

The front door swung open and Sienna appeared, separated from them by the screen door. She was beautiful, hair pulled back in a messy topknot, dressed in a fuzzy sweater and blue jeans. Her feet were bare. Red polish coated her toenails.

Eli's heart skipped a beat. Their conversation in the church had been raw and vulnerable, but it'd filled him with hope. No matter what happened with Dalton, Sienna would walk through it with him. So would his fellow rangers. And God. Eli wasn't alone, and that small comfort gave him the strength to approach this situation with an open heart and mind.

"Dalton, there you are. Come in out of the cold." She pushed the screen door open, a smile bunching her cheeks. "Hope you came hungry."

"I did." Dalton hugged her.

Henry, the family Labrador, stood at Sienna's side. The dog greeted Dalton with a lick to the back of the hand as he entered the house before shifting to Eli to demand more attention.

He obliged, stroking the dog's ears. Then he leaned over and kissed Sienna's cheek. Her eyes sparkled with joy, but there was a touch of concern buried in their depths. Worry for him. And Dalton.

Leila exited the kitchen, followed by Wyatt. They both greeted Dalton with big hugs. Landon, Sienna's brother, shook his hand.

At one time, his brother had been a part of their family. Before he relapsed into addiction, before Eli broke up with Sienna. It was amazing how quickly they all fell into old patterns. Eli and Dalton set the table while Landon arranged extra folding chairs. Sienna helped her mother finish the last meal preparations, and Wyatt made sure everyone had something to drink.

Sunday dinner was a staple in the Evans household, and pretty soon, extended family arrived. They poured into the house with kids and food and conversation. It was loud. It was chaos. But it was warm and homey and everything Dalton and Eli hadn't grown up with.

He'd missed it. More than he'd let himself admit to before now. This farm... this family... Sienna. They were the things he wanted for his future. He wanted to raise his children around people who loved and cared for them.

Eli glanced at the beautiful woman by his side. He'd spent the last five years without her but was determined to spend the rest of his life with her. It was too early to discuss forever—Eli needed to prove that he was a changed man—but his intentions were set.

He prayed Dalton would be a part of that future.

The next several hours were spent eating, laughing, and swapping stories. Sienna's giggles never failed to make Eli laugh too, which sent pain shooting through his midsection thanks to his cracked rib. But he didn't mind. It'd been a long time since he'd seen her happy. It was nice to set the case—and the worries—aside for a while. Even Dalton seemed to have a great time. He and

Landon were the same age and spent most of the evening catching up on each other's lives.

Finally, after dessert and dishes, when most of the extended family had left, Dalton pushed away from the table. "It's getting late, and I should head home. I have work tomorrow morning." He turned to Leila and Wyatt. "Thank you for everything."

"Come back and see us." Sienna's mom hugged him. "There's no need to be a stranger."

"Yes, ma'am." Dalton shook Wyatt's hand, said goodbye to everyone else, and shrugged on his jacket.

Eli followed him onto the porch. The screen door slapped closed behind him. "Mind if we chat for a minute?"

"No. In fact, I was going to ask you the same thing." Dalton shifted in his boots, as if gathering his courage, and then let out a breath. "I owe you an apology. The way things ended between us... I was messed up and made some terrible decisions. It took me a long time to realize how much I'd put you through and I'm sorry for all the pain I caused. You should also know I'm not that person anymore. It doesn't change the past, but I hope you can find it in your heart to forgive me."

"Of course I can. If you'll forgive me." Eli took a deep breath and let it out slowly. "I failed you, Dalton. Dad's abuse and Mom's depression shaped us. It made me hyper responsible. It made you reckless. We were both hurting, but I failed to recognize that your bad choices were born out of that pain." He met his brother's gaze. "I'm not saying it was wrong to draw healthy boundaries around our relationship, but I am sorry for not supporting you when you made the right decision to seek help."

Tears glittered in Dalton's eyes and he swiped at them. "Bro, you gotta stop now. I'm not gonna cry like a baby on the Evans' porch. Talk about embarrassing."

Eli laughed. "You always were a softy."

"Better than being an emotionless robot." Dalton went to punch his midsection, but froze, fist midair. "Oh yeah. I can't hit you after those guys beat you up."

"Jerk."

"Loser."

They embraced. This time, there was nothing awkward about it. For the first time in a long time, Eli had his brother back. A love he couldn't describe stole his breath. He didn't think about the case. Or the charity. Or the money laundering. Instead, a thousand childhood memories flooded through him. Helping Dalton with his homework, building a fort to hide in when their dad came home drunk, tossing a baseball around in the empty field behind their house.

They shared a bond that was unique. Eli had never had a child, but the love he felt for his brother was close to it. He'd raised Dalton. Being estranged had created a hole in his heart no one else could fill. Eli wanted to freeze this moment when everything was right between them.

Dalton backed away. "All right. We got all the touchy stuff out of the way. How about we go to a ball game next week? I'll get the tickets."

"Can I tell you in a day or two?" Eli glanced behind

him at the house. "Things with the case aren't settled, and until they are, I don't have any free time."

Dalton touched his head with the heel of his hand. "Duh. Of course." He leaned against the railing. "Are y'all still looking for Jesse O'Neal? I saw on the news that he's a person of interest."

Eli's dinner swirled in his stomach as a sour taste filled his mouth. He didn't like the direction this conversation was taking. "Yeah. Why?"

"I was Jesse's counselor at Fresh Start. He's been through a lot of rough stuff over the years, which led to his addiction. I'd hoped he'd stay sober and keep out of trouble this time. He did well for a while before all of this happened." Dalton's voice was layered with sadness. "It's never easy to see someone with so much potential make such bad choices."

Eli could sympathize with that sentiment. He'd felt the same about Dalton. "Do you know of any place Jesse would hide out? It's important we find him." He gauged how much to tell his brother. "We believe he's in trouble with the same guys who kidnapped me and Sienna."

Dalton considered the question for a long minute. "Jesse doesn't have any family in this area, and he's a loner. Off the top of my head, I can't think of where he'd go, but if I hear from him, you'll be my first call."

"Thanks."

Eli watched his brother bounce down the steps and get into his sedan. The taillights winked as he hit the brakes at the end of the driveway before turning toward town.

He planted his hands on the railing. A mixture of emotions swirled inside him like a typhoon as old fears flared to the surface. He'd been trained to always prepare for the worst. This time, he didn't want to.

The screen door creaked open and then slammed shut. Sienna appeared next to him. She wrapped an arm around his waist. "Are you okay?"

"I will be as soon as this case is over." He turned and pulled her into his arms. The world felt better with her close by. "We talked. I apologized for not being there when he needed me. It was good. I don't know where things go from here, but I've decided to believe in his innocence. Maybe that's foolish. I don't know. Dalton's made plenty of mistakes in the past, but so have I. He's my brother. I want to believe in the best of him."

"That doesn't sound the least bit foolish to me." Sienna pulled back to look him in the face. There was no recrimination or judgment in her expression. Instead, there was pride. "You've changed, Eli."

"I promised I'd prove it to you."

"You're off to a great start."

Eli tilted his head and captured her mouth with his. Her lips were soft and feminine, yet she matched his passion with the same intensity. She pulled him closer in silent invitation to deepen the kiss. He didn't disappoint. His breath stalled as his heart tumbled over and over in his chest. Nothing existed outside of this. His entire world narrowed to this beautiful woman and the way she made him feel.

When the kiss ended, they were both breathless. Eli

pulled her back into his arms, and Sienna rested her head on his chest. They stood there for a long time as the rain pattered against the porch roof. It was freeing to finally release the fear he'd carried around for as long as he could remember. To trust. To believe.

He was strong. He was capable. And God would see him through.

Sienna's cell phone rang, breaking the moment. She pulled it from her jacket pocket and glanced at the screen. "I don't know who this is." Frowning, she hit the answer button. "Hello?"

"It's Jesse. We need to talk."

TWENTY-THREE

Sienna parked her car on the side of the road. Her windshield wipers worked overtime to combat the downpour. It'd been an hour since Jesse's call. He refused to tell her anything on the phone, insisting they meet in person. She had the sense the man was terrified.

He also claimed to know where Ruby was.

"This is a terrible idea." Eli dipped his head to study the two-story warehouse in front of them. The building had long ago been abandoned. Busted windows gaped like empty eye sockets. Hunks of plaster and brick had broken off, littering the area immediately in front of the building with debris. A rusted metal fence surrounded the property, but vagrants had cut holes looking for an escape from bad weather. "We don't know how many people are in there or if Jesse is telling the truth about knowing where Ruby is. This could be a trap."

"How far away are Cole and Ryker?"

"Twenty minutes." He glanced behind him at the empty street. The rangers were chasing down a lead in the next county, and although they headed back to Sandalwood immediately following the call, the weather slowed their response time. "I think we should call Chief Ramirez."

"No way. Jesse will run at the first sign of law enforcement. Besides, we have no idea who's involved in this scheme. The last thing I want is our only lead to be killed by someone we think is a good guy, but is actually working with the Greer brothers." She tapped her thumb against the steering wheel. "I wasn't even supposed to bring you, Eli."

He scowled. "You are not going in there alone."

"Understood, but as it stands now, the minute Jesse sees you, he may bail." She sighed. "He's terrified. With good reason. This is our chance to convince Jesse to tell us who's in charge of this entire operation and find out where Ruby's being held. We have to take the risk."

Her cell phone rang. Jesse.

Sienna answered the call.

"I can see you sitting in your car." His tone was hostile and suspicious. "What's taking so long? If this is some kind of trick—"

"It's not a trick. I'm getting out of the car right now." Sienna opened the SUV's door. Rain pelted her in the face, but she didn't lift the hood on her raincoat. Jesse was already tense enough. This was no time to make the situation worse by shielding her face. "See? Here I am."

Eli opened the passenger side door and got out.

"Who's that with you?" Jesse's voice rose in panic.

"It's Eli."

"I told you no cops!"

"You need protection, right?" Sienna shouted so her voice carried over the sound of the rain. Her hair was plastered to her head and droplets ran down the back of her coat into her collar. A thick river of water followed the curve of the sidewalk as it raced to the sewer grate at the end of the block. She hurried toward the broken gate surrounding the warehouse. "Eli has connections. He can provide a safe house and make sure no one finds you."

Jesse didn't answer. For a heartbeat, Sienna feared he'd hung up on her. Then the sound of his rapid breathing fired in her ear. If he was pretending to be scared, the man was delivering an Oscar-worthy performance.

Eli held open a broken part of the fence, and Sienna slipped through it. Her boots slid on the wet grass. "We're coming in. Where are you?"

"Second floor."

Jesse hung up.

Lightning streaked across the sky, followed by a pounding clap of thunder. Fear streaked down Sienna's spine as she reached an entrance to the warehouse. The door was cocked open, the interior pitch-black. Fighting back her instinct to run away, she waited for Eli to catch up, and then slipped inside.

The door slammed closed behind them.

The stench of sweat, decades of fish, and saltwater smacked her in the face. The far side of the warehouse was exposed to the ocean. Boats would bring their catch straight inside and unload. Ancient equipment, rusted from disuse, hunched like goblins in the darkness. The only light came from a fire burning in a metal trash can. Sleeping bags rested nearby, but there was no sign of their owners.

Still... someone had been here. And recently, otherwise the fire would've burned out.

The whisper of a boot scraping against the concrete floor sent Sienna's heart rate stuttering. She whipped off her raincoat. It dropped to the ground in a puddle of plastic. Sienna removed her handgun from its holster, but kept it pointed at the ground. These warehouses were prime real estate for the homeless. Most of them were harmless.

Then again, they could be friends of Jesse's.

Eli had also removed his weapon from its holster. His gaze swept their surroundings. "Lead the way. I'll cover you."

She nodded and then headed for the staircase on the right. Her footsteps were silent. Sienna adjusted the hold on her weapon. It felt slightly foreign in her hand after days of not carrying. Since the murder charges against her were dropped, she was no longer required to adhere to the bond requirements. Her Glock was still in evidence since it'd been used to kill Albert, but her father carried the same weapon. She'd borrowed his before leaving the house and was thankful for the extra protection.

The staircase was cement. Sienna raised her weapon and traversed the first few steps, going slowly enough that if someone took a shot at her from above, she'd have time to react. Eli stayed close. His constant and solid presence was reassuring. There was no one she trusted more to keep her safe.

The second floor was darker than the first. A shadow moved along the far side of the wall. Sienna swallowed back a gasp and whirled toward it.

A match fired up, illuminating Jesse's face for a second, before a kerosene lamp flared to life. "Don't shoot me."

She lowered her weapon but didn't holster it. Icy air whipped through the building from the exposed wall below and goosebumps broke out across her skin. The upstairs space must've been used as an office when the warehouse was in operation, based on the dirty desk in the corner.

Eli joined her on the landing. As one, they moved farther into space, closer to Jesse who was leaning against the far wall. A sleeping bag, a portable camp stove, and a pile of alcohol bottles crowded the small room. In his hand, he held a pistol but kept the weapon loosely positioned at his side. Judging from his filthy jeans and sweat-stained shirt, he hadn't showered in days. Dark circles hung under his eyes.

"My grandfather used to own this building." Jesse's voice was hollow. He crossed the room toward the window on the other side of the office. Sienna moved to keep him in full view while still maintaining access to the stairs. "We had money back then. Lots of it. But then business started going south and when my dad took over, he lost everything. He started drinking. Using drugs. That's how I started." He laughed, but there was no mirth. "My dad was my first dealer."

Sienna didn't understand where Jesse was going with the story, but she sympathized with him. "My sister was an addict. My parents tried to help her but couldn't. It was devastating. I can't imagine what it's like to be pushed into it by someone who's supposed to protect you."

He turned to study her in the dim light. "So you understand. I'm an addict, but I'm not a bad person."

He broke into an elderly woman's home and attacked her, but now was not the time to debate morals. Sienna kept her tone even and hushed. "Where's Ruby, Jesse?"

He gestured for her to come closer. She didn't dare glance at Eli but trusted that he'd stand back. Dust and grime coated the floor. Sienna's heart pounded as she took a few steps toward Jesse. The stench of alcohol poured from him, and she almost gagged. His pupils were dilated. He was drunk and high.

He pointed out of the window at the warehouse next door. "She was there, but I've been watching for the last hour, and there's been a lot of movement. I think Gideon is packing up the operation to move it somewhere else. I don't know if Ruby's still alive."

Sienna's breath caught. "Gideon? He's behind this?"

It made sense. As the director of Fresh Start, Gideon had access to the donations and the invoices, and could launder the money that came from drug sales. "He hired you to break into Ruby's house."

"Yes, but I wasn't the one who attacked you in the marina. And I didn't kill Albert." He moved around her, quick as a rabbit, and blocked the stairs. He raised his weapon and pointed it at her. "I was going to turn you into Gideon. He wants you dead, but I figured it wouldn't save me. He'd kill me after he killed you."

Eli already had his weapon pointed at Jesse. "Put down the gun."

Jesse ignored him. He locked eyes with Sienna. Resolve was etched on his features. "Save Ruby if you can and tell my mom that I did the right thing in the end."

Jesse turned the gun and lifted it to his own head.

Sienna held up a hand. "No! Don't!" Panic spiked her heart rate. Jesse had made terrible choices, and he deserved to pay the consequences for them, but suicide wasn't the answer. She was relieved when he hesitated and took the opportunity. "There's a better way out of this."

Eli moved closer, but Jesse reacted by pointing the gun at him and taking a giant step toward the stairs. "Don't do it, cowboy." His breath came in puffs. "You can't protect me. No one can. Gideon has friends in high places, and the moment he figures out I've turned on him, then I'm dead."

Footsteps on the stairs shot fresh adrenaline through Sienna's veins. Eli pointed his gun at the approaching figure, as did Jesse.

Dalton appeared, and his complexion paled as he took in the scene in front of him. He raised his hands. "What's going on?"

"What are you doing here?" Eli growled.

"I thought about what you said earlier tonight about Jesse needing a place to hide." He locked eyes with his former patient. "I remembered your grandfather used to own this warehouse and took a chance."

"Go away, Dalton." Jesse held the gun back to his own head. "It's over."

"No, it isn't. I can help you." Dalton took another step closer. "But first you have to put the gun down."

Jesse's whole body trembled. "I can't... Gideon..."

Dalton's eyes widened in surprise at the mention of his boss, but to his credit, he didn't shift his attention away from Jesse. "You don't need to fear Gideon. He'll be in prison."

"He's sneaky—"

"Doesn't matter. My brother is the best Texas Ranger in the state and he's never let me down. Not once. If Eli promises to do something, he follows through." Dalton didn't take his gaze away from Jesse but directed his next question to his brother. "Isn't that right, Eli?"

"You have my word, Jesse."

Tears filmed the man's bloodshot eyes. Sienna held her breath as Jesse's hand wavered as he started to lower the weapon from his head. Then he whipped it back up. "I'm sorry. I can't."

Dalton lunged for him, grabbing Jesse's hand and wrestling him for the weapon. Sienna and Eli both bolted across the space to help.

The gun went off.

TWENTY-FOUR

Eli slapped the handcuffs on Jesse's wrists. Adrenaline and fear made his fingers tremble as he gripped Jesse's arms and pushed him into a seated position against the wall. "Don't move." Anger pulsed through his words. "Don't even so much as blink, you understand me?"

Jesse sobbed, his gaze fixed on Dalton's prone form a few feet away. "I didn't mean to shoot him."

Eli ignored him, whipping off his jacket and then his flannel button-down, before dropping to his knees next to Sienna. She was using her hands to stop the flow of blood, but the move was ineffective. Eli gently pushed her out of the way so he could apply pressure with his shirt. "Sienna, call 911."

She swiped her hands on the legs of her pants, leaving smears of blood on the fabric, and then reached for her cell phone. Rain pounded against the roof of the warehouse in a rapid beat that mingled with Jesse's cries from across the room. Dalton was still conscious, but his complexion was pale. Sweat beaded on his forehead.

Dalton grimaced as Eli pressed hard on his wound. "Hurts."

"I know. I've been shot in the gut. But I survived and you will too." Eli half-listened as Sienna spouted off the information to dispatch. Ryker and Cole were in route, but by his calculations, they were still a good ten minutes away. And neither of them had the medical equipment necessary to stabilize Dalton for transport to the hospital. They needed an ambulance. "Help is coming. You just have to keep breathing."

"Gideon..."

"Is going to prison for drug smuggling and money laundering." Eli kept talking to distract his brother from the excruciating pain. "He's been using Fresh Start as a cover for his illegal activities. We think Ruby figured it out, and he kidnapped her. When Sienna started investigating, Gideon got scared. He's been trying to prevent us from putting the pieces together."

The director had murdered Albert for blackmailing him and framed Sienna for it. He'd sent his thugs to burn down Sienna's house with her in it, run them over with a speedboat at the marina, and kidnap them from the parking lot of Fresh Start. He'd even hired Jesse to break into Amelia's house to steal Ruby's computer. All so Gideon could keep smuggling drugs into the country on the Trident IV, with the help of the Greer brothers, while laundering the gains they earned from the drug trade through a nonprofit charity designed to help addicts stay clean.

It was diabolical. Heinous. But it all made sense.

Except for one thing... why kidnap Ruby? Why not kill her?

"You..." Dalton puffed, sweat pouring from his brow. "You suspected I was involved, didn't you?"

"For a moment." Eli kept the pressure on. His arm muscles trembled with the effort. "You had access to the invoices and the donations. But I never really suspected you."

"I knew. From your face... when I asked about Jesse." His mouth contorted with pain. "But you still apologized to me. Why?"

"Because I was wrong. I meant every word I said to you on the porch." Tears pricked his eyes as a prayer winged from his heart. He didn't want to lose his brother. Not like this. Not when they'd found each other again and had begun the hard work of healing old wounds. "I should've protected you better. And treated your mistakes with kindness and compassion. I'm so sorry."

"Don't... don't be." Dalton's skin grew paler by the second. He was losing too much blood. "You were the best brother. So perfect. You did everything right. I couldn't measure up."

"That's not true. You're braver than me. Fearless. You literally flung yourself at an armed man to stop him from committing suicide."

He smiled weakly. "Yeah, but I got shot."

"It's okay. We'll have matching scars."

Dalton huffed out a laugh and then grimaced.

Sienna appeared at Eli's side. She dropped the phone on the floor next to his knee. "Dispatch is on the line and an ambulance is en route." She brushed the damp hair away from Dalton's forehead with a gentle touch. "Hang in there."

"Doing my best."

She met Eli's gaze. "Ruby may still be alive, but there isn't much time if Gideon has initiated his escape plan. I have to try to save her."

Panic sent Eli's pulse skittering. He wanted to order her to stay and wait for backup, but it was a selfish desire. Like Dalton, Sienna was fearless. She put others before herself every time. And her sister's murder haunted her. Harper's death had created its own scars on Sienna's heart, and she lived with regrets about it every day.

If Ruby died while Sienna stayed here waiting for backup, she'd never forgive herself.

Eli knew all of this without being told a word. Sienna was a part of him, and he understood her better today than he had five years ago. "I love you."

"I love you too."

She leaned over and kissed him. It was fleeting and softer than a feather, but the emotion behind it could've powered the entire city.

Then she was gone, the sound of her footsteps pounding on the stairs before fading into the night.

Dalton attempted to sit up. "Go with her!"

"NO!" Eli shoved him back down and reapplied pressure to his wound. "If I leave, you'll bleed out before help arrives."

"You... can't.... let her go alone."

"She isn't." Eli sucked in a breath, pressing harder on his brother's gunshot wound. Fear wanted to steal his words, but he knew the truth buried in his heart. "Sienna isn't alone. She's going with God."

Then he prayed. For Ruby. For Dalton.

And for Sienna, the love of his life.

TWENTY-FIVE

Icy needles of rain pelted Sienna's face as she raced toward the warehouse at the end of the block. Paint peeled from the facade and metal bars covered the windows. On the left side, a truck bay door was partially open, the bottom of a white van barely visible. Someone was definitely inside.

Sticking to the shadows, she circled the building, searching for a back way in. Her breath came in ragged puffs and her heart felt like it was about to beat out of her chest. Every inch of her clothing was wet. She was frozen to the bone and didn't have a game plan formulated on what to do once inside the building, but kept moving forward anyway. If there was a chance to save Ruby's life, she had to take it.

There! A side door. Sienna tested the knob and discovered the door was unlocked, the wood warped by time and the weather so that the latch didn't catch anymore. She paused. No sound emanated from inside, but it was hard to hear over the sound of the rain. Sienna purposefully flexed her fingers around the handgun to loosen her muscles. She needed to be prepared for anything.

Darkness beckoned as she slipped inside the warehouse and eased the door closed behind her. Sienna gave her eyes a moment to adjust. Cranes and boxes littered the space. Long industrial assembly lines had been pushed to one side. Voices filtered from her right. Water droplets coated the floor as Sienna moved in that direction, using whatever she could find as cover.

The rear of the van came into view. Luis Greer stood hunched over inside, arranging boxes in the back with the skill of a professional mover while other men moved back and forth, handing him items. Sienna recognized some of them from her tour at Fresh Start. Her stomach churned. Gideon hadn't just used his charity as a cover for his drug trade, he'd also used it for recruiting workers. The man was a monster.

But where was Ruby? There was no sign of the young woman.

A small office sat to the right. Could she be in there? Sienna started moving in that direction and Gideon came into view. He was stationed at a card table, a computer in front of him, weighing something on a scale and then separating it into baggies. Drugs. Probably heroin.

"Hurry up." Gideon stood and closed the box, indicating one of his workers should tape it shut. "We don't have much time. This entire warehouse needs to be emptied tonight."

Luis hopped out of the back of the van. "We'll have to do another run. We won't be able to move all the product left in one trip."

Sienna's eyes bulged at the number of boxes lining the far wall. There had to be several million dollars of drugs in the warehouse. At least five armed men, including the Greer brothers, were within striking distance and there was no sign of Ruby. What was she doing? If she was caught now, they'd kill her.

Fear swiftly stole her breath. Her hands trembled. Eli's colleagues, Ryker and Cole, were en route, but would they arrive in time to help her if she got into trouble? Probably not. She was on her own. And she'd left Eli behind, caring for his shot brother. He wouldn't be able to leave until the ambulance arrived. And even then, his mind would rightfully be on his injured sibling. It would take time for help to arrive.

This was foolish. Reckless. There wasn't any proof that Ruby was even alive. But if Sienna left now, and she discovered that Ruby had been killed afterward, she'd never forgive herself.

God, have I made a terrible mistake? She warred with herself, uncertain about whether to continue forward or retreat. *What do I do?*

The door to the office opened and Tony Greer appeared. The bulky man had someone by the arm and hauled the person out of the office and into the main room of the warehouse. Slender. Dark hair.

Ruby!

She was dressed in ill-fitting clothes and shoes too big

for her feet, but she was alive. Sienna's heart leapt at the sight of the young woman, but her relief was short-lived when Tony shoved Ruby to the ground. She cried out. None of the men seemed to care.

Tony turned to Gideon. "What do we do with her?"

He sneered. "She's a loose end. It's time to snip it."

Desperation swelled inside Sienna as Tony unholstered his handgun and took aim. Ruby began pleading for her life. Her terrified cries were heartbreaking. Sienna had to do something. Shooting Tony wouldn't do a lick of good and it would identify her location. She couldn't help Ruby if she was killed in the process of saving her.

Sienna's gaze swept the ground, landing on a nearby wrench. It was rusted and broken, but it would do the trick. She lifted the item and threw it across the warehouse. It clattered against the cement.

Gideon whirled. "What was that?"

Every man in the place aimed a weapon toward the noise. Lightning lit up the sky, leaking into the warehouse through the large windows overhead. Sienna spotted another heavy duty screw. She wrapped her fingers around it, preparing to use it as another distraction. It wasn't a good plan, but it was better than nothing. If she was lucky, the men would lock Ruby back up to conduct a search of the warehouse. That would buy time. Maybe enough for Ryker and Cole to arrive with backup.

Air shifted behind her one second before the barrel of a gun touched the back of her head.

TWENTY-SIX

"Drop your weapon."

Sienna hesitated, but she had no choice but to obey.

Her gun clattered to the cement floor. The noise revealed her location to the rest of the men in the warehouse. In a flash, she was staring down the barrel of several guns. Some long-buried survival instinct silenced every one of her emotions. She was numb inside, even as her mind snapped into incredible focus.

The man holding her at gunpoint grabbed her arm and forced her to move forward, roughly manhandling her until they were close to Ruby. Then he pushed her. Sienna landed on the hard ground on her knees, and pain vibrated through her body.

She barely felt it. Her attention landed on Ruby's tear-stained face. Terror poured from the young woman. Sienna took her hands, giving them a squeeze of comfort before shifting to face the person who'd snuck up on her.

Dallas Redding.

A thousand questions rolled through Sienna's head, but she shoved them all to the side. Figuring out how Dallas fit into Gideon's band of thugs wasn't her priority.

She needed to figure out an escape plan. With Ruby.

Gideon gaped like a fish out of water. "How did she get in here?"

"You weren't careful. Fortunately, it appears she's alone." He smirked in Sienna's direction before turning toward Gideon. "What are you guys doing?" He assessed the situation with a flat stare. The van. The boxes. The men. Icy anger, more dangerous than anything Sienna had ever witnessed, emanated from him. "You aren't thinking of bailing on our agreement, are you?"

Ruby trembled. Sienna shifted, drawing closer to the other woman, sensing her fear was rising exponentially. It seemed impossible considering Tony was about to shoot her a few moments ago, but her complexion was pasty and the whites around her eyes were showing.

Her gaze was fixed on Dallas. As if he was the source of her growing horror. Then she shifted her attention to Sienna. A flash of remorse flared in the depths of her eyes, as if she knew Sienna would pay the ultimate price for trying to save her.

"I'm not going to prison for this." Heat rose in Gideon's face, turning his complexion red. "Law enforcement is close to figuring everything out." He pointed to Sienna. "Obviously, she did. And that ranger she's been working with can't be far behind. We need to change the plan."

Dallas arched a brow. "Interesting. When were you going to tell me about this grand new plan?"

"I just did," Gideon snapped.

The men faced off. Ruby gripped Sienna's hands in hers. Her skin was cold and clammy. Bruises in the shape of fingerprints marred the skin on her neck. At any other time, Sienna would've been horrified by them, but right now, her brain couldn't process those emotions. She had to focus on an escape plan. Could she use the fight between Gideon and Dallas to her advantage?

"Watch your tone, Gideon. I control the cartel in South America. Without them, you don't have a product to sell. More importantly, do you really think you can stab me in the back and live to tell the tale?" He flipped a glance at the men in the room and they all cowed, like dogs tucking their tails between their legs. "Any of you?"

The warehouse was silent. Rain beat against the windows and the roof. No one dared to take a breath.

Sienna's mind whirled. Dallas was the one in control of the drugs, not Gideon. They were partners. Dallas provided the product, while Gideon handled the logistics. It would explain Dallas's "sailing" tours. He probably used his boat to help bring drugs to US shores, along with the Trident IV.

She suspected Dallas Redding wasn't the man's real name. From the way the men reacted to his threats, Dallas must be deeply embedded in a wider criminal organization. Maybe even related to a drug lord.

Gideon's face grew redder. "Don't threaten me or my men." He jabbed a finger toward Ruby. "Your obsession with that woman set all of this in motion. If you had just listened to me and let her be—"

"SHE'S MINE!" The roar erupted from Dallas like a volcano. He reared back and punched Gideon in the face.

The sound of cartilage breaking preceded Gideon's cry of pain. He doubled over, hitting the ground on his hands and knees. Sienna took advantage of the distraction to scooch herself toward the darker recesses of the warehouse, pulling Ruby with her. Any moment, law enforcement was going to storm the building. She and Ruby needed to be as far away from these criminals as possible.

"You broke my nose!" Gideon's voice was muffled as he glared up at Dallas. He dropped his hand away from his face and rose to his feet. "You're going to pay for that."

"I don't think so. Where's the rest of the product? Where did you move it to?"

Gideon's hand balled into fists and he shook with rage. "Tony. Luis. Dallas is the one who killed your cousin, Albert."

Sienna stifled a gasp. The air in the room shifted as Tony and Luis processed that tidbit of information. In two seconds, both men had a gun trained on Dallas. Rage twisted their features.

Chief Ramirez had been right. Nothing was more important to the Greer brothers than family. Not even when faced with the threat of being hunted down by a cartel.

Where were Ryker and Cole? What on earth was taking them so long?

It felt like an eternity had gone by since Sienna entered the warehouse, but it must've only been a few minutes. She hadn't even heard the wail of an ambulance. Had anyone reached Eli and Dalton yet? Her stomach clenched at the thought that Eli was desperately trying to save his brother's life, but couldn't. She prayed the thunderstorm had masked the approach of the ambulance and Dalton was getting the help he needed right at this moment.

She also prayed for Ryker and Cole to hurry.

And for God's protection.

Sienna squeezed Ruby's hand and caught her gaze. She tilted her head toward the shadows to show where they should move toward. To her relief, Ruby gave a slight nod. The younger woman was terrified, but she still had her wits about her. That was good. It would make running for their lives easier.

Leading the way, Sienna shifted her weight and slid across the concrete. Ruby followed. No one paid them any attention. Every thug in the room was focused on the drama playing out between Gideon and Dallas. And now the Greer brothers.

Luis stalked closer to Dallas. "You killed my cousin?"

Dallas raised his weapon and pointed it at Luis, but it was useless. He was flanked by the Greer brothers and couldn't possibly kill them both. "Gideon's lying. What reason would I have for killing Albert?"

Sienna shifted again, bringing Ruby with her.

More. A little more. They weren't out of range of the gunfight and this situation was set to explode. One wrong move and someone would fire.

"You killed Albert because he was blackmailing us." Gideon was bent on spilling all of his secrets. "You promised to take care of the problem, but you only made it worse." He took a step back and lifted his chin. "Tony and Luis, we don't need him anymore. The cartel knows us now. Why continue to give Dallas the bulk of our earnings when we're the ones doing all the work?"

Dallas shifted his gun toward Gideon. "Shut up, before I kill you."

Luis and Tony shared a look. The brothers were criminals, but they weren't stupid. Both of them had caught on to Gideon's confession. He'd been in on Albert's murder. At the very least, he'd known about it.

Sienna's pulse elevated as she shifted to the balls of her feet, gesturing for Ruby to do the same. Things were about to get very ugly.

Luis lifted a brow, an angry smirk on his face. "Why do we need either of you?"

Suddenly, the entire warehouse was plunged into darkness.

The storm? Or the rangers? Either way, it was a chance at escape.

Sienna bolted to her feet, dragging Ruby with her. She pushed the young woman out of the line of fire as gunshots erupted.

TWENTY-SEVEN

The hospital waiting room was a bustle of activity. Ambulances pulled into the covered bay, rushing past with injured patients. More people waited in plastic seats to be seen by a doctor. A television played quietly in the corner. Eli, his clothes wet from the rain and spotted with his brother's blood, sat in the corner. He held Sienna's hand in his, but his gaze was locked on the doors leading to the interior part of the hospital.

Dalton was in surgery. He'd coded in the ambulance, according to reports Eli received when he arrived. No one knew if his brother would make it.

His leg jittered. "Waiting is the worst."

"I know." Sienna tucked her other hand in the crook of his elbow and leaned on his shoulder. "Can I get you anything? Coffee? Or something to eat?"

"No." He turned his head and kissed her forehead. Eli couldn't imagine putting anything in his stomach. It was tied up in knots. But he appreciated the gesture,

216

especially since she'd been through her own terrifying experience tonight. She and Ruby had survived the gunfight that transpired after Eli and his colleagues killed the electricity to the warehouse prior to storming it.

Dallas was dead. So was Tony Greer. Luis and Gideon, along with the rest of their cronies, survived and were currently sitting in the county jail. Crime scene investigators were combing through evidence at the warehouse and Fresh Start. It would take a while to put all the pieces together, but Eli doubted any of the men arrested tonight would ever see the outside of a prison cell when it was all said and done.

The sliding doors to the hospital swished open. Cole and Ryker hurried in, bringing with them a blast of cold air. Both men were damp from the rain and dirty from the raid on the warehouse. They caught sight of Eli and Sienna, beelining straight for them.

"Any news?" Cole asked. He sported a scuff on his chin from tackling Luis, and the leg on his pants was torn at the knee.

Eli shook his head. "Not yet."

Ryker placed a reassuring hand on Eli's shoulder. "Dalton's strong and healthy. He's also a fighter. Like his big brother. Goodness knows it takes more than a bullet to the gut to take down either of you guys."

He stood and hugged his best friend. "Thanks."

Cole hugged Eli as well. "The rest of Company A is on the way. And Grady's wife initiated the prayer chain. You've got extended family and friends all praying for Dalton to pull through."

Grady West was another one of their colleagues. His wife, Tara, had taken it upon herself to create a special group chat for prayers. More than one of the members of Company A had been injured in the line of duty. Over time, the prayer chain extended to family and close friends.

Eli was touched by the support of his teammates. Sienna's family was also in the waiting room. Leila, Wyatt, and Landon had parked themselves in the chairs next to Sienna's. He was surrounded by love. And community. It was all he'd ever wanted as a child, and despite the fear swirling his insides, Eli knew he was truly blessed.

A doctor pushed open the swinging door and entered the waiting room. "Hutchinson family?"

Eli's heart skipped a beat even as he jumped forward. "That's me." Sienna caught up to him and he took her hand in his, welcoming the support and love she gave so willingly. "I'm Dalton's brother."

"The surgery went well. He lost a lot of blood, and it was touch and go there for a while, but he's stable now. He needs to stay in the ICU for the next day or so, but barring any complications, he should make a full recovery."

Eli sagged with relief. "Can I see him?"

"Not for a while. We're still getting him settled. A nurse will come and get you in a bit."

The next few minutes were a blur as the doctor told him more about the surgery and then his friends and

Sienna's family hugged him. Finally, he was able to have a moment with the woman he loved.

He pulled her into his arms and took his first deep breath since entering the warehouse to meet Jesse. "It's all going to be okay."

"Yes, it is."

Their sweet moment was interrupted when Chief Ramirez and Lieutenant Rodriguez entered the waiting room. Eli stiffened at the grim looks on their faces. "Is Ruby okay?"

"She's fine." Vikki reassured him. "Or as well as she can be, considering she was kidnapped and held by Dallas for weeks. Ruby is an impressive young woman. She paid attention to everything and has helped to fill in the blanks of our investigation."

The chief scraped a hand through his hair. "Turns out Dallas Redding wasn't his real name. It's Dallas Vega."

Eli inhaled sharply. "Of the Vega cartel?"

"One and the same." Vikki caught Sienna's confused expression and explained. "The Vega cartel is a powerful crime family in Nicaragua. They're connected to many crimes abroad and in the US. Dallas wasn't high in the network, but he had enough of a connection to build an empire in Sandalwood and the surrounding counties. The Vega family supplied the drugs through Dallas. They were smuggled into the US on Dallas's yacht. Eventually, business got big enough, they bought the Trident IV."

"Gideon's job was to recruit dealers who would

distribute the drugs," Sienna said. "And to launder the money once it came in."

Vikki nodded. "Precisely. The relationship between the two men started off fine, but disintegrated over time. Dallas's obsession with Ruby was the final straw. Gideon figured out she discovered the money laundering and wanted to kill her. Dallas refused. He kidnapped her instead, and sent someone who worked for him to different areas of Texas to take money out of ATMs using her debit card. That way authorities would believe she'd simply skipped town. The plan was to smuggle her out of the country during their next drug tradeoff, but the shipment was delayed."

Eli squeezed Sienna's hand. "That's the shipment Tony and Luis were talking about."

"Thank goodness for that delay. Otherwise we might never have found Ruby." Sienna turned to Vikki. "How did Ruby get a hold of a cell phone?"

"She found a burner phone the men used to avoid detection during drug trades in the warehouse and called her grandmother. She was short on time and tried to tell her about the file on her computer, but got cut off."

"That's why it took us so long to figure out she'd uncovered the money laundering."

"Yes. In the meantime, Albert began blackmailing Gideon and Dallas. He knew what the men were up to because of his cousins. He threatened to tell you, Sienna, about Ruby if they didn't pay him. Again, Gideon wanted to kill Ruby, and then use Tony and Luis to silence their cousin. But Dallas refused. He was incensed

Albert had the audacity to blackmail him. He came up with the plan to kill Albert, but framed you for the crime."

"Two birds." Eli's jaw clenched. "One stone."

Chief Ramirez shook his head. "Again, I'm so sorry for not believing y'all. I should've investigated Ruby's disappearance and Sienna's claims of innocence more carefully."

Eli agreed with that assessment, and judging from the look on his boss's face, so did she. Vikki wasn't the kind to let sloppy police work slide. She'd joined forces with the chief to get the job done, but now that the case was coming to a close, he was sure there would be some conversations about changes that needed to happen in the Sandalwood Police Department.

Sienna grimaced. "If Dallas was involved in the attacks against me, why did he come to our rescue at the marina?"

"He wasn't responsible for that attack," Vikki explained. "That was Gideon. The house fire, the speedboat, kidnapping y'all... Gideon was trying to stop the investigation. When the attack at the marina happened, you had just interviewed Dallas. He was worried you'd figure out he was involved somehow."

"So he played the hero to convince us he was innocent," Eli concluded. "It nearly worked."

"Thanks to you both, it didn't." Vikki gave them a beaming smile. "You busted an entire drug operation and saved Ruby's life. Pretty impressive for a week's work."

"Don't expect the same next week." Eli winked at her. "I'm still on medical leave."

Everyone laughed. Then Vikki's expression grew serious. "Ruby is asking for you guys. I know it's been a long night, but—"

"We'd love to talk to her." Sienna glanced at the doors leading to the interior section of the hospital. "What room is she in?"

"Eleven."

Eli shook his boss's hand, as did Sienna. Then they made their way to Ruby's room.

The young woman was sitting up in bed, covered by a hospital blanket and a homemade quilt. Amelia, her grandmother, held her hand. She released it to rush Sienna, embracing her in a hug.

"Thank you." Tears streamed down Amelia's face. "You brought my Ruby back to me."

Eli's own throat clogged as Amelia hugged him too.

Ruby gestured for them to come closer. She looked exhausted, but it didn't diminish the beauty of her smile. "Lieutenant Rodriguez explained everything you both did for me." She reached for Sienna's hand. "I can't thank you enough."

"You don't need to thank us." Sienna gave her a hug. "Seeing you here with your grandmother is thanks enough."

They chatted a bit more with Ruby, but once her exhaustion became more obvious, they slipped out of the room.

Eli wrapped an arm around Sienna's waist and tucked her close. "You're amazing, you know that?"

"We're amazing." She hip-bumped him. "It was a team effort."

"Yes it was, but if you ever put yourself in that kind of dangerous situation again, I'm going to hog-tie you to a chair on the farm."

She came to a stop in the middle of the hallway. "You wouldn't dare. Unless you're willing to stop hunting killers and take a nice desk job at some boring office." She poked him in the stomach, very close to his bullet wound. "I'm not the only one with a dangerous job."

There was no arguing with that. Still... he cupped her face. "I don't want to live without you, Sienna."

"Ditto." She gazed at him with so much love, it made his breath hitch. "But we aren't guaranteed tomorrow, no matter what our jobs are. The only thing we have is right now." Her gaze dropped to his lips. "So I suggest, Ranger Goodwin, that you make the best of it."

"Yes, ma'am."

He kissed her.

TWENTY-EIGHT

Three months later

Sienna ran down the porch steps and flung herself into Eli's arms. He swung her in a big circle before placing her on her feet and then kissing her softly. His touch was like the air she breathed. Necessary. Sienna's arms twined around his neck, her fingers dipping into the soft hair at the nape, silently inviting him to kiss her more.

Eli didn't disappoint. By the time he pulled back, Sienna's heart pounded against her rib cage like she'd ran a marathon and she was breathless. He looked equally stunned. Their passion wasn't new, but a bolt of pleasure shot through her knowing that everything she felt, he did too. "Hey there."

He grinned. "Hi."

It'd been a few days since they last seen each other. Eli had been investigating a double homicide a few counties over. Dark circles shadowed the skin under his eyes, a testament to the long hours he'd put in, but it didn't detract from his good looks. Her heart skipped several beats just being near him. "I missed you."

"Missed you too." He lightly kissed her nose.

"Did you catch the bad guy?"

"Yep." His smile faltered. "Mind if we talk about the case later? I want to forget about everything for a while."

She completely understood. His work could take a toll, as could hers. "Absolutely." Sienna glanced at her watch. "In fact, we should get going. We're supposed to be at Fresh Start to help set up at two."

After Gideon's arrest, Fresh Start closed its doors. It took time for all the legal paperwork to get sorted, and for Dalton to recover from his gunshot wound, but Eli's brother was determined to reopen the charity's doors. Today's fundraiser would go a long way to making that happen. And with Dalton as the charity's director, Sienna knew it would be a success.

She hesitated, thinking about how the last few days had been hard on Eli. "Unless you don't feel up to it. I'm sure Dalton will understand if you need to cancel—"

"No way." Eli reached for the passenger side door. "I've been looking forward to the carnival fundraiser all week. Some fun, friends, and silly games are exactly what I need right now." A shadow crossed his face, and he swallowed hard. "We need to make a stop on the way there though."

"Sure thing. Where?"

"You'll see."

Sienna's brow wrinkled as she climbed into the vehicle. Curiosity begged a thousand questions, but she held them back. Eli didn't particularly like secrets or surprises. She was interested to see what he had in mind. From the nervous way he fiddled with the air-conditioning vent before firing up the truck, he was upset about something. Maybe it had to do with the case?

Or maybe it had to do with them?

Oh heavens, was he going to break up with her?

No, that was a silly thought. Since getting back together, they'd fallen deeper and deeper in love. Conflicts arose, but unlike they'd done in the past, Sienna and Eli talked them through. True to his promise, he'd approached every problem with kindness and compassion. It'd made it easier for Sienna to express her true feelings about things. The result was a stronger, deeper, and more lasting love.

Eli steered the truck toward her parents' farm. Sienna rolled down her window, letting the spring sunshine and the scent of flowers into the cab. Together they sang along with a country music song on the radio, eventually dissolving into laughter. Some of the tension riding Eli's shoulders evaporated, and he looked less tired than he had when arriving at her place.

Suddenly he flipped on his blinker and turned into the Hendersons' driveway. Sienna frowned. "What are we doing here? Do you need to help Mr. and Mrs. Henderson with something?"

The elderly couple had lived next door to her parents' farm for Sienna's whole life. They had three grown children and a gaggle of grandkids, but for the last several months, the beautiful ranch house had been empty. Mr. Henderson had fallen and broken his hip. The couple had temporarily moved to Waco to be closer to their daughter so she could help them.

"Not exactly." Eli parked and killed the engine. "Let's take a walk."

"On the Hendersons' farm?" Now she was really confused.

Eli didn't answer her. He simply circled the truck and opened her door.

Sienna hopped out, trying to figure out what on earth was going on. Her inquisitive nature couldn't let things be. "You're being very mysterious."

He took her hand and led her to the house. Sunflowers danced in the overgrown flower beds. A set of rocking chairs rested in the corner of the wide front porch. In the other corner, an oversized swing beckoned for someone to take a rest with a glass of sweet tea and a book. A grove of pecan trees grew next to a brook that weaved itself along the edge of the property. It was like something out of a story book. Sienna had always loved this place.

Eli licked his lips as he turned to face her. "The Hendersons contacted me last month. They've moved to Waco permanently to be closer to their daughter and grandkids."

Sienna felt a pinch of sadness. "Oh... I'm sorry to see them go, but I understand it's what's best for them." She frowned. "Wait. Why did they call to tell you this?"

"Because shortly after you and I got back together, I paid them a visit and explained that if they ever decided to sell their property, I wanted to be their first call. Since I know how much you love this house, I didn't want to miss the opportunity to buy it."

Her mouth dropped open. "You're going to buy the Hendersons' property?"

He shifted nervously in his boots. "I already did." Eli reached into the pocket of his light jacket and pulled out a small jewelry box before lowering to one knee.

Sienna gasped and tears filmed her eyes.

"Sienna Marie Evans, I want to build a life with you. I know we've been engaged before, and it all fell apart, but this time, things are different. I've changed. You've changed. We've grown and become better. Every day, I fall more and more in love with you, and there's no one else I'd rather grow old with. Please, will you marry me?"

Tears streamed down her face and emotion clogged her throat. Sienna, unable to get the words out, nodded.

Eli slipped the beautiful engagement ring on her finger before gently wiping her tears.

She hugged and kissed him, her heart full. "I can't believe it. How did you even think to buy this property?"

"Well, for starters, I knew how much you loved it. And your parents and brother are our neighbors. We'll be surrounded with love and support, and if one day we're blessed with kids, they'll be close to family." He cupped her face, worry clouding his features. "You're not mad I bought it without asking you first, are you? If this doesn't make you happy, we can sell it—"

"It makes me very happy." She kissed him with all the love swelling inside her. "You make me happy."

An hour later, they arrived at Fresh Start. The charity was still housed in the original warehouse, but the surrounding area was improving. It turned out the company who'd purchased a large swath of the warehouses was owned by Gideon. His family put them up for sale to raise money for his lawyer's fees.

It hadn't made a difference in court. Gideon was convicted of his crimes and would never see the outside of a prison cell. However, the sale of the properties meant actual businesses purchased the old buildings and could do something useful with them.

Restaurants and stores lined both sides of the street. It never failed to fill Sienna with joy to see this area of town bustling with excitement. Especially since Ruby handled most of their advertising and marketing. The young woman's harrowing story of survival had inspired many people. Residents gathered together to make her dream of opening a marketing business a reality. While she still had a long road of recovery ahead of her, Ruby was thriving.

With God's good blessings, and some hard work, so would Fresh Start. The setup for the fundraising carnival was already in full swing when Sienna and Eli arrived. Every ranger in Company A was there. Several arranged tables and chairs. Others were assembling booths. Dalton ran from place to place, solving problems and helping where it was needed.

Jesse trailed behind him with a clipboard. The former criminal had gone to an intensive rehab program and committed to do thousands of hours of community service. Sober, Jesse was thoughtful and kind and endlessly helpful. He'd apologized to everyone he'd hurt, including Ruby's grandmother. Surprisingly, the two of them had lunch every week and often sat together in church. She had become something of a surrogate parent to him.

Sienna lightly elbowed Eli. "We're late. How embarrassing."

"No one will give a hoot once we tell them the reason for it."

His assessment was spot on when most of the setup was finished and the group had gathered around the refreshment station for a small break. Sienna was deep in conversation with Ryker's wife about the trials and joys of pregnancy when Hannah suddenly grabbed Sienna's left hand.

Her eyes bulged as she took in the diamond. "What is this?"

Sienna couldn't keep the smile from her face. "That's why we arrived late for the setup." She glanced at Eli. A warmth filled her insides at the love shining in his eyes. "Eli asked me to marry him and I said yes. We're engaged." Sienna turned back to Hannah. "Again."

The crowd cheered. The next few minutes were spent hugging, discussing the engagement ring, and accepting well wishes. Sienna's head spun by the time the group had dispersed, leaving only Dalton.

He hugged Sienna. "Welcome to the family. You deserve a medal for putting up with this lug for the long haul." He shoved Eli. "Don't screw this up, man. You won't find better than her."

"I'm aware."

Eli hooked an arm around his brother's head and tilted him down so he could muss up his hair. That move earned him a jab in the midsection with Dalton's elbow as he twisted free. The two men laughed.

Sienna rolled her eyes at their antics, but was secretly overjoyed at how close they'd become. Eli was incredibly proud of his brother. Dalton was honest that addiction was a lifelong struggle, and there was always the chance he'd be tempted to use again, but he had the tools to reach out for help if it came to that. And Eli would be one of his first calls.

Dalton was flagged down by a staff member, and he left with a smile and a wave, smoothing his hair into place as he strolled to the stage.

Eli and Sienna rejoined the small group at the refreshment table. Ryker had his arm hooked around his wife's waist as they chatted with Cole. The group greeted them.

Eli wagged his eyebrows at Hannah and said, "I need your help. Please convince Sienna that a wedding can be planned in a few months."

"Months?!" She smoothed a hand down her protruding belly. Hannah and Ryker's baby would be born in the fall. "Are you worried she's going to get cold feet, Goodwin?"

"Absolutely. She might come to her senses and realize marrying me is a bad idea. I gotta get her to the altar before then."

Sienna lightly smacked his shoulder. "Stop it. Marrying you is exactly what I want to do." She winced. "But planning a wedding is a lot of work. My mom has been making the guest list since Eli and I started dating again. I'm afraid this is going to turn into a production and there's no talking my parents out of it."

"You don't have to be the bad guy. I have a fantastic wedding planner. She knows just how to handle parents and extended families and any other problem that might come up." Hannah leaned closer to her husband. "She did our wedding, and there wasn't a single hiccup. I can't recommend Olivia enough."

"No offense, guys." Cole grabbed a soda from the refreshment table. "But wedding talk is where I bow out."

He marched away on long strides. Sienna watched him go and then glanced at Eli. "Is he okay? I know this stuff can be boring, but he seemed irritated."

Eli shrugged. "A lot of the rangers in Company A are married now. I think Cole feels like an endangered species."

Ryker gazed down at his lovely wife. "All of us find the right one eventually. Cole will too."

Sienna wasn't sure Cole wanted to be in a relationship. He was supportive of his friends and their marriages, but she sensed he kept anyone remotely interested in dating him at arm's length. A pity. He was a great guy. Smart, loyal, and a good friend. Any woman would be lucky to have him in her corner. Sienna often wondered why he wasn't interested in finding someone, but she hadn't wanted to pry. Cole would tell her one day if he wanted to.

The music kicked off as guests arrived for the carnival. Volunteers manned the food stations and children squealed with excitement at the smell of hot dogs and cotton candy. Sienna and Eli ran one of the game booths for an hour, laughing at players' antics as they attempted to pop a balloon with a dart for a prize.

"Everyone is having a great time." Sienna relished the feel of Eli's hand in hers as they strolled toward the funnel cake station. She jutted her chin toward the stage, where a tally of the night's donations were displayed on a giant whiteboard. "Looks like Fresh Start surpassed their fundraising goals. Dalton will have enough to restart all the programs they previously offered. I'm glad."

"So am I." His gaze took in their surroundings. "This is the kind of community we'd always wished for as kids. A place to call home where we're surrounded by people who care about us."

She gently squeezed his hand. "You are home. Both of you belong here."

Eli pulled her to a stop in a quiet corner of the fair, wrapping his arms around her waist. "Have I told you how much I love you today?"

"You have, but I never get tired of hearing it."

His sky-blue eyes shimmered with so much warmth

and affection, it made her breath catch. Sienna couldn't believe this wonderful man would soon be her husband. Their future would have ups and downs, but together, they could get through anything.

"I love you." Eli brushed his mouth against hers. "More than I can find the words to say."

She rose on her tiptoes to kiss him back. Her heartbeat quickened and her insides turned to molten lava. This man unraveled her, and would for the rest of her life. "I love you too."

ALSO BY LYNN SHANNON

Texas Ranger Heroes Series

Ranger Protection

Ranger Redemption

Ranger Courage

Ranger Faith

Ranger Honor

Triumph Over Adversity Series

Calculated Risk

Critical Error

Necessary Peril

Strategic Plan

Covert Mission

Tactical Force

Would you like to know when my next book is released? Or when my novels go on sale? It's easy. Subscribe to my newsletter at www.lynnshannon.com and all of the info will come straight to your inbox!

Reviews help readers find books. Please consider leaving a
review at your favorite place of purchase or anywhere you
discover new books. Thank you.

Printed in the USA
CPSIA information can be obtained
at www.ICGtesting.com
LVHW050443111224
798841LV00010B/166